THE
Valet's Secret

THE
Valet's Secret

PROPER ROMANCE

JOSI S. KILPACK

SHADOW
MOUNTAIN

Visit us at shadowmountain.com

This is a work of fiction. Characters and events in this book are products of the author's imagination or are represented fictitiously.

Library of Congress Cataloging-in-Publication Data

Names: Kilpack, Josi S., author.
Title: The valet's secret / Josi S. Kilpack.
Other titles: Proper romance.
Description: [Salt Lake City] : Shadow Mountain, [2022] | Series: Proper romance | Summary: "Kenneth Winterton and Rebecca Parker find a second chance at love when they unexpectedly meet on a country road. But Rebecca, who is from the work-ing class, is unaware that the valet who has captured her heart is actually the heir to the earldom. When the truth is revealed, will she give Kenneth another chance? Romance blooms in this story of second chances and secrets with a double Cinderella twist."—Provided by publisher.
Identifiers: LCCN 2021045305 | ISBN 9781629729893 (trade paperback)
Subjects: LCSH: Man-woman relationships—Fiction. | Valets—Fiction. | Mistaken iden-tity—Fiction. | Nobility—Great Britain—Fiction. | BISAC: FICTION / Romance / Historical / Regency | FICTION / Romance / Clean & Wholesome | LCGFT: Romance fiction. | Historical fiction.
Classification: LCC PS3611.I45276 V35 2022 | DDC 813/.6—dc23
LC record available at https://lccn.loc.gov/2021045305

Printed in the United States of America
Lake Book Manufacturing, Inc., Melrose Park, IL

10 9 8 7 6 5 4 3 2 1

Dedicated to everyone who is wanting, fearing, and hoping for a second chance.

Chapter One

I f Kenneth Bartholomew Winterton had learned anything in his life, it was that there were things a man could live without and there were things that were entirely essential. For instance, a certain routine had been necessary when he had been in active service to the Crown, but upon leaving the Royal Navy, he'd learned that a set schedule was not all that important—he could sleep late if he wanted to, or not sleep at all if he was of a mind.

It had become essential since returning to a gentleman's existence, however, to hone his manners in ways the military had not demanded of him, including hiding the fact that one of his favorite hobbies was sketching—a decidedly feminine talent. Though he'd had to hide that when he had been in the king's service as well.

For the most part, Kenneth could look back on his forty-eight years and feel reasonable pride at how well he had adapted to the different turns his life had traversed by evaluating what to let fall by the wayside and what to apply his time and attention toward.

Someone yelled from outside the carriage, and Kenneth came back to the starting point of his meandering thoughts—essentialism—and to the conversation that had put him in this carriage, on this road, at this inn, considering what aspects of his independent life he could let go of once they reached Wakefield, and which parts he would absolutely need to find a way to keep.

"I shall leave no mystery as to the reasons for my demands that you come to the estate, Kenneth," Uncle Lester, the fifth Earl of Brenston had said at Christmas. "It is time for you to join the society here and choose a wife from the local gentry to help establish your position."

It had taken Kenneth six months to settle his affairs in Sussex, but the further changes his life would take still stumbled like a lame horse in his head when he allowed his thoughts to dwell there. He had not been raised to be the heir to his uncle's title or the community position that came with it. That had been the role of his cousin. But Edward had died unexpectedly two years ago without a legacy, and according to the laws of heraldry, Kenneth's circumstances had, in that moment, markedly changed. He was no longer just a landowner of a small estate in a southern county, but an heir to an earldom in the north with duty and responsibility beyond himself.

Uncle Lester had taken great care in educating him through letters and occasional visits about what this new position required—exact protocols, studious intention, flawless behavior, and complete respect for his place in the history of their nation.

Oh, and finding the right wife.

With two sons nearly grown, Kenneth did not need marriage to procure an heir for himself. But Uncle Lester had explained that those living in such northern villages struggled to accept those not born among the rugged hills. Marrying a woman with solid roots in the area, who could facilitate the right introductions and host the proper social events, would make all the difference in securing his position. Kenneth could accept that such a marriage was a reasonable idea—but was it *essential*?

According to Uncle Lester, it was.

Kenneth had agreed to Uncle Lester's expectations on principle but was feeling trepidation as the abstract idea was rapidly becoming his reality.

The carriage door opened, and Kenneth's valet slid inside, shutting the door tightly behind him. Malcolm was out of his coat by the time Kenneth finished pulling the curtains closed. Kenneth hurried to similarly shed himself of his skin, as it were.

Just for a little while.

"Meet us at the stone wall west of the church on Barnsley Road," Malcolm said. "It's a simple parish church on the outskirts of the village. The man at the inn made it sound as though that would be an easy enough marker to identify. If you reach the cathedral, you have gone too far."

Kenneth nodded both his understanding and agreement while shrugging into Malcolm's coat—an unadorned gray tweed that would help with the disguise.

Malcolm tossed his hat, and Kenneth caught it, placing it

on his nearly bald pate. He kept his head shaved to spare him the stubble—he had a nicely shaped head—and wore hats as often as possible, though not this sort of shapeless felt thing that Malcolm favored.

Kenneth pulled the wide-brimmed hat down to his ears and finished settling the coat on his shoulders—it was a bit snug—while Malcolm put on the dark-green greatcoat that would mark him as Kenneth for the next two hours should someone glance inside the carriage.

Kenneth did not know what he would do without Malcolm. They had served together in the navy, and though their life circumstances had been different—Kenneth a gentleman and Malcolm a tailor's son—saving one another's lives a handful of times had put them on equal ground. After his uncle's estate fell upon his shoulders, Kenneth had asked if Malcolm might be willing to help him with the adjustment. He needed a valet, and, more importantly, a friend who understood him and would help him fill the uncomfortable shoes he'd been given.

Upon their arrival at Brenning Hall later that afternoon, Malcolm would take his place in the servants' quarters, while Kenneth took his place in the tower bedroom—his favorite part of the house.

Some of the best memories he had of his younger cousin, Edward, had been playing in the tower room at the top of the spiral stairs. They had both loved the remoteness of the room and had had grand adventures amid the storage trunks and abandoned furnishings.

When Uncle Lester had told Kenneth it was time for him

to permanently relocate himself to Brenning Hall, Kenneth had asked if he could take the tower room as his bedchamber. Uncle Lester had argued that Kenneth should be in the family wing, but Kenneth had essentially begged until he won. There would be similar arguments about hunting and playing cards that Kenneth was not sure he would successfully argue, so he took great comfort in this victory.

In the carriage, coats and hats in place, the two men traded boots—few things defined a man as well as his footwear. Within another minute, the head-to-toe transformation was complete.

"This is reckless," Kenneth said, opening the curtains and feeling the thrill of getting away with something. After all, Uncle Lester expected him to arrive starched and pressed in a carriage.

"Indeed, it *is* reckless," Malcolm said, leaning against the cushions. "But in comparison to the cannon fire, Continental invasion, and three-month-old biscuits aboard a ship, such as we have known, pretending to be an ordinary man so that you might gallop through the country against your uncle's wishes seems rather mild."

"Oh, I do appreciate your powers of justification, Malcolm." Kenneth took one more look around the yard to ensure no one was paying attention. "Thank you. I shall see you at the stone wall."

"That you shall, you mangy dog." Malcolm settled further against the cushions, clearly prepared to take a nap.

Kenneth chuckled, then opened the door and jumped out, doing his best to emulate his friend's stride. The horse that

Malcolm had procured from the posting inn, a rouncy, bay-colored gelding, was tethered to the post beside the carriage.

The carriage driver was still gossiping with the stable hands on the other side of the yard, so Kenneth lifted a hand to wave at the driver with his face averted, then patted the horse, introduced himself, and swung into the saddle. The bay stamped in place and snorted in protest.

"Easy," Kenneth said, patting the horse's flank and glad to have a spirited animal. So often, the rented horses were docile creatures without much fire. Malcolm had chosen well.

Though Kenneth would be living in his uncle's house and learning to manage his uncle's land, perhaps even marrying the woman of his uncle's choosing, Kenneth was determined to retain his *self-ness*. It was not that he was ungrateful for the bounty that had come his way—far from it. He had purpose and position most men dreamed of, but there had to be room for both Kenneth Bartholomew Winterton and the heir presumptive to the title of Earl of Brenston and everything that role required.

Kenneth tapped his heels into the sides of the mount, expecting the animal to move forward smoothly, only to find himself clinging tightly to the horse's mane when the animal whinnied and reared back onto its hind legs.

"Whoa," Kenneth said, dividing his attention between maintaining his balance and making sure no one approached to offer help.

The carriage driver turned his direction, spurring Kenneth's determination to get out of the yard, regardless of whether this particular horse was a wise choice or not. If there was any hope of keeping up his disguise as Malcolm, it had to get off to a solid start. To be discovered during his very first attempt would be pure ruination!

Kenneth braced himself as he dug in both heels, barely keeping his seat as the horse lunged ahead with incredible force.

"Gracious," Kenneth said as he leaned forward against the horse's mane and clenched the reins tightly. Fear for his life kept him tight against the horse's back for some time, until the wind began to pull the worries from his mind like the last few leaves on a vine in autumn. He relaxed slightly and let the horse take its head, feeling the energy of the animal course through him.

Wide open country.

Solitude.

Freedom.

Remembering who he was and what he loved.

This was essential.

Chapter Two

Rebecca tried not to stare at the gilt picture frames adorning the walls or the velvet-covered chairs balanced on tiny legs that did not seem strong enough to hold a child, let alone grown adults. The idea that her work—well, officially Father's work—would be displayed on these walls was incredible, and she felt the tingle of it all the way to her toes.

She'd never been past the foyer of Brenning Hall before today, and the company parlor was every bit as beautiful as she'd expected it would be.

Father shifted beside her and she recentered her focus. Father wasn't particularly good with clients, which was why Rebecca usually handled the initial meeting. But Lady Beth had asked to meet with the artist himself, and no one refused Lady Beth.

"Why can you not do the sitting here?" Lady Beth asked, her incredibly thin and incredibly dark eyebrows pulled tightly together at the bridge of her nose.

Did she ink her eyebrows? Rebecca wondered. Who thought of such things?

"My studio has the screen and lighting arranged for the best possible shadow contrast, a necessary element for a good silhouette," Father said.

His tone was even and professional, thank goodness. Rebecca did not think he'd had anything to drink today, which accounted for the slight tremor in his hands, but which also kept him from crossing into one of his increasingly foul tempers.

Lady Beth blew out a breath of ladylike frustration. "Surely you can bring your equipment here," she said, her tone a demanding whine. "The west drawing room can accommodate everything you need for as long as you need it. And it gets excellent light. When Giuseppe painted my portrait last spring, he proclaimed the room absolutely perfect; the best exposure he'd seen in Yorkshire."

"That is the exact trouble," Father said, rubbing his hands on the knees of his best trousers, though they looked shabby in comparison to the room decorated in gold and green accents that fairly sparkled in the afternoon light. And this wasn't even the west drawing room that Lady Beth had referred to.

Brenning Hall was the finest home in Wakefield and nearly twice the size of Grangeford—where Rebecca had once been on staff and still helped with the occasional dinner party. It had gas lights in the ballroom and, rumor had it, the kitchen had been modernized with a water pump. Rebecca had never seen the kitchen, of course; in fact, until today, she had never stepped past the foyer, but she believed every word of the rumors.

9

"A silhouette is done in a darkened room, with positioned lighting that allows a crisp outline." Father's tone was getting tighter.

"In the dark!" Lady Beth put a hand to her neck, the skin pale and smooth thanks to a lifetime of covered carriages and parasols.

Rebecca and Lady Beth were near the same age, and they had attended the same parish church as girls, though their situations had kept them apart in every other way. Rebecca had left school to go into service when she was fourteen, while Lady Beth, Lord Brenston's only daughter, had gone to finishing school where she became well-versed in French and the harpsichord and a dozen other topics that had no bearing on Rebecca's life.

The expectation had been that Lady Beth would find herself a fine husband, but the village had let out a combined gasp when Mr. Marlow—a landowner of some fortune—began paying her attention just one year after his wife had died. Mr. Marlow had been thirty years' Lady Beth's senior when they married, and she had been nearly a decade younger than his grown children.

Such marriages happened amid the noble classes, of course, but not often in this part of Yorkshire. The marriage had lasted ten years and produced three daughters before Mr. Marlow died and his eldest son inherited his land. Though it was rumored that Lady Beth had been left a good legacy by her husband, she had returned to her father's house and brought her daughters with her—the Brenston granddaughters, as they were known collectively within the county, even though their surname was Marlow. When Lady Brenston had become ill, Lady Beth had seamlessly taken over as hostess for Brenning Hall, easing the transition for when Lady Brenston passed a few months later. Lady Beth had been the mistress here for five years now.

"Certainly you do not expect me to bring my daughters to a dark studio to sit for a portrait? The very idea is—"

"It is not a portrait," Father snapped, his neck beginning to redden. "If—"

"It is a silhouette, Lady Beth," Rebecca interjected before he could say something she could not resolve. "A cutout of the outline of your daughters in profile. The studio must be dark, then lit from in front of them so that their shadow is projected upon a paper set upon the wall. The sitting shall require half an hour for each girl. You are invited to be in attendance, and I shall be there as well."

"I just do not understand why it cannot be done here," she said, her tone becoming more crisp. "The west drawing room—"

Father stood so abruptly that Rebecca startled from her position beside him on the settee.

"This is the work I do, madam," he said sharply. "You may inform us of your decision by messenger once you have made your choice." He turned and began to walk out of the room without having been excused.

Rebecca came to her feet, holding the portfolio of silhouettes that they had reviewed upon arrival. Lady Beth had chosen a full body shade, which would be reduced to half the actual body size of each girl.

Lady Beth rose to her feet as well, her eyes wide with surprise as Father strode toward the door. Walking out of an interview in the earl's household was simply not done.

Rebecca turned from Father's retreating back to Lady Beth, who looked as aghast as Rebecca felt.

"Forgive my father," Rebecca said, keeping her voice soft and her manner mild in hopes of balancing Father's rudeness. "As I know you have worked with many exceptional artists, perhaps you are also familiar with an artist's temperament?"

"Of course," Lady Beth said after a few moments, casting an uncomfortable glance at the doorway through which Father had disappeared. She turned her piercing gaze on Rebecca. "We always sit for portraits here in the house, Mrs. Parker. To entrust my daughters elsewhere is against my nature."

Rebecca nodded her understanding and then explained—for the third time—the process of a silhouette, which was not, in fact, a portrait or a sculpture or a sketch. It was an outline, drawn upon paper, then transposed into another medium—silk, paper, wood, plaster, leather, or even shell. The work was an inexpensive opportunity to create a person's likeness and was quite popular among the middle class. It had only been in recent years that the upper classes had expressed interest in the "folk" art. It was an exciting prospect to work with someone of Lady Beth's position.

"Well, I just don't know," Lady Beth said, clasping her hands tightly together. "I'm sure my father would not approve. Lord Brenston is even more particular to propriety than I am."

"I would be happy to explain the process to Lord Brenston when he is available, and you are both welcome to visit my father's studio any time, as well as stay for the sittings, of course. I assure you the process is entirely respectable, and the work will be of the highest quality. Thank you for inviting us today. Good day, Lady Beth."

Lady Beth managed a farewell, and Rebecca was escorted to the door by one of the footmen, who then helped her into Father's carriage.

Father had been a carpenter since his youth—adding detailed flourishes to upscale furniture mostly—a skill he'd learned from *his* father. He'd tried his hand at shades nearly twenty years ago only to find he had singular skill. He had first carved miniature likenesses from ivory or shells that were then set upon coral and fastened to a clasp to make a cameo pin, and then transitioned into the flat-screen silhouettes that were so affordable and easy to display within people's homes.

It had always been a secondary occupation for him, but then last year he had done a life-size silhouette of Mary Langley—Lady Beth's cousin—that now stood framed in the Langley home. He'd received more interest from the local gentry since then, and he'd been able to give up the carpentry, which had become more difficult to do as he'd aged. His free time, however, had taken him to the pub more often, which had done nothing to improve his already negative disposition.

The carriage door had no sooner closed when Father began his ranting, and Rebecca felt her insides tightening in response. "How dare she make such accusations of—"

"She did not accuse anything," Rebecca cut in.

"And she expects me to dismantle my entire studio and move it to her home? As though she is my only client?"

"She does not understand what her request entails, Father. I'm sure once she saw the studio, she would understand that it is not an option."

"As though my home is beneath her, and she is more deserving than anyone else for accommodation!" His hands sliced the air as he spoke, and Rebecca looked out the window as the tension continued to build.

Rebecca had returned to Father's house when her husband, David, died eight years ago because she could not keep the rooms herself; their daughter, Rose, had only been eleven years old at the time. Returning to a home that had not been a happy one when she was growing up had been a difficult decision—Father was not an easy man—but her only other option had been returning to service. Now that Rose was grown and employed, it was harder and harder for Rebecca to withstand Father's abuses. A change would need to be made, but that frightened her too.

When the carriage reached the road, Rebecca hit the ceiling with her hand to signal the driver to stop.

Rose was meeting her today, and they would have time to walk into town together before Rose had to return to her work as the baroness's companion at Grangeford. It was a good position, and Rebecca was proud of her daughter for earning the elderly noblewoman's compliments and trust.

Instead of getting used to Rose's absence, as Rebecca expected she would, each month had become more difficult. Rebecca found herself lonely in ways she had never been before, and she often felt vaporous in the world she had always lived in, as though she could disappear and no one would notice. Sometimes she felt the need to cling tightly to anything that brought comfort or pleasure, and other times she feared that doing so would only make her miss the lack all the more strongly when it was gone.

The carriage began to slow, and Father stopped midsentence. "What is this?"

"I am walking the rest of the way," Rebecca explained. She slipped her reticule over her wrist, though it held nothing of substance, and made sure the portfolio would not slide to the floor of the carriage without her holding it in her lap. "I told you I would be meeting with Rose after our appointment today."

Father harrumphed and shook his head. "That is ridiculous." Small beads of spittle emphasized the words. "I am not finished!"

He was never finished.

"I shall be home in time for supper." She'd started a stew that morning and had left it simmering in the coals.

He narrowed his eyes, but she ignored the look and focused on exiting the carriage. Father said something more, but she closed the door behind her without hearing the words which she knew would not be kind.

"Thank you, Stevens," she said to the driver, who was also their man of all work and cared for the horses. His wife was their housekeeper and cook. Stevens nodded and wished her well before snapping the reins to get the two horses moving forward again.

Rebecca stood off to the side of the road until the dust settled, then removed her bonnet and lifted her face to the sun, letting the warmth wash through her.

She would never have the smooth and blemish-free skin of Lady Beth. She *would*, however, enjoy the simple pleasures of life as often as she could. She knew from experience that such things were often fleeting.

"All is well," she said to the buzz of the bees and slight rustling of the trees that sounded like the finest orchestra.

She turned from the road to the footpath that cut through the woods abutting the Brenston estate, tapping her bonnet against her leg and letting the ribbons dangle freely. This was when she felt the most content—alone on the path that would take her to Rose. She would forget her loneliness, her discomfort at home, her concern for Father's moods, and every other worry that usually nipped at her heels. For now, she would just be Rebecca and find joy anywhere she could take it.

Sun on her face.

Breeze in her hair.

Time all her own.

Freedom.

Chapter Three

Freedom sometimes came at a very dear price, and as the horse took a turn far too fast, Kenneth was not sure the freedom was worth what he'd paid. The horse was a menace! A rather exhilarating menace, but a menace still the same, and though Kenneth had enjoyed the gallop through fields and country, he desperately needed the beast to mind him now that they were on the road nearing the village. Did the animal not know how to trot?

The stamina *was* impressive, however, and maybe with a bit of ground training—

A flash of blue cloth and a woman's scream cut his thoughts short.

Kenneth's eyes met the wide green ones of the woman in blue half a second before she dove for the side of the road and out of the horse's path. He pulled hard on the reins, which caused the horse to wheel in a circle, but with no less energy than displayed on the rest of the journey. The animal lunged forward, nearly unseating Kenneth yet again as it continued down the road.

It took nearly a quarter of a mile before the horse finally obeyed Kenneth's command to stop. He successfully turned the horse back the way they had come but was afraid to spur a run for fear the animal would not stop until it reached the next county. Kenneth instead jumped from the saddle and pulled the horse with him as he ran back down the path. His heart was racing as he came around the bend and saw the woman in blue standing at the roadside, brushing off her skirts. If she'd been dressed in gray or brown, he might not have seen her at all. Wearing blue may have saved her life.

"Oh good, you are unharmed!" Kenneth said with relief as he crossed the remaining distance.

The woman straightened and turned to face him, eyes flashing with green fire that brought him to a stop. "Unharmed! I have just pulled myself out of the bushes, thank you very much! What on earth are you thinking, riding like that on a public road! What if I had been a child? Or an elderly woman? Good gracious, have you no decency at all?"

Kenneth stared at the woman, who looked as though she wanted to bludgeon him with the crushed bonnet she held by the ribbons in her tight, white-knuckled fist. He had not been spoken to this way since leaving the navy and never by a woman. "I, uh, I rented this horse, and it has a mind of its own."

She rolled her eyes and huffed a breath as she looked away from him. That was when he noticed an angry scratch along her jaw and a tear in the sleeve of her dress, through which he could see the linen of her shift. Her hair was disheveled and tangled with small sticks and leaves. Goodness, she *had* feared for her life, hadn't she?

"I am very sorry, ma'am," he said. "How can I help make it right? Do you need a ride to the village?"

She looked at him again, eyes still flashing. "You are offering me a ride on a mount you cannot control?"

"Uh . . ."

She turned away. "I am fine. Good day, sir."

She limped slightly as she began to walk away from him. He hurried to catch up, reins in one hand, while digging his handkerchief from his pocket.

"You're hurt," he said. "Let me fetch a doctor."

"I am fine," she said tightly.

"You are limping, and the scratch on your face looks painful."

She stopped and turned toward him while lifting a hand to her face. When her fingers touched the scrape, she winced slightly. He was ready with the handkerchief and held it out to her. She looked at it a moment before taking it and pressing it to her cheek.

The gurgle of a nearby creek offered an opportunity to try to make up for what he'd done. What if she *had* been a child or elderly woman? He felt suddenly grateful that the harm done was only a scratch and a sprain.

"You should sit down, ma'am." He put a hand at her elbow, and she let him guide her to a rock that she could sit upon. The fire had gone out of her so quickly that he worried about the fast turnabout. She might be experiencing shock.

"Let me wet that for you in the creek." He held out his hand, and she looked at him as she handed back the handkerchief.

"Thank you," she said.

Kenneth noted a few small spots of blood upon the cloth. "I am so sorry."

He wrapped the horse's reins around a nearby tree branch, and the horse obediently bent its head to eat the grass at its feet. Kenneth scowled at the animal who was the source of all this trouble and then hurried in the direction of the water, necessitating that he navigate a rather steep bank before he reached the stream. He soaked the handkerchief, wrung it out, soaked it again, and then hurried back up the embankment.

The woman in blue looked paler than she had before, making the scratch stand out even more garishly upon her face. The injury did not seem to be terribly deep, but it stretched almost from her ear to her chin.

He folded the handkerchief into a compact rectangle before pressing it against the woman's injury, putting his other hand on the opposite side of her face to hold it steady. She was shaking slightly, her eyes seeming to stare past him at nothing in particular.

"I think you are experiencing a bit of shock, ma'am, which is to be expected," he said. "Take a deep breath and hold it inside your chest for the count of four, like this."

She focused on his eyes and followed his instruction as he breathed along with her for several breaths.

The color in her face improved slightly, and with it, the realization descended upon Kenneth that he had not been this close to a woman—had not touched a woman in any way other than to bow over her hand—in a very, very long time. He had not looked this closely into a woman's face for . . . He could not remember the last time.

Lydia, his late wife, had been gone nearly fifteen years now. They had only been married long enough to have their two sons, and she had died while he was at sea. After leaving the king's service and returning to his children, Kenneth felt sometimes as though Lydia had never existed at all, save for the reflection he saw in his boys; they'd had so little time together.

He'd considered remarrying in the years that followed, but courting had felt like a monstrous chore when the boys were young, and he'd not encountered a woman who sparked his interest. He instead developed his land to be as profitable as possible with crop rotation and managed a significant renovation of the house, barns, and tenant housing. He'd allowed a mining company to work the west portion of his land, and he'd expanded his sheep since the textile industry was growing so rapidly.

When he had become heir to an earldom, women seemed to appear around every corner, which he found rather offensive, and he avoided women more than ever. And yet, here he was, inches from a woman and feeling something both strange and familiar.

This woman in blue was not young, but neither was she old—forty years perhaps? And their unusual encounter had not included any of the usual pretense that had colored every other exchange he'd had with a woman for the last two years.

There were fine lines around her eyes, and a furrow across her forehead, yet her eyes were bright, and her lips were full, and though he'd been taken aback by her anger in the beginning, the passion behind that anger was rather invigorating. He was used to a gentler version of the female sex. This woman was different. Perhaps because he'd nearly run her over, but still, the difference intrigued him.

When Kenneth realized he'd been staring far too intensely for far too long, he forced his eyes away from her face. There was a leaf in her blonde hair; he'd not have noticed the few strands of silver had he not been so close. With the hand he had been using to steady her face, he removed the leaf, then smoothed the tangle in her hair as best he could, which was not very well at all.

She was watching him when he met her eye again. Without saying a word, she took hold of his wrist and directed his hand back to her cheek. Then she closed her eyes and took a deep breath.

He knew exactly what she was doing: relishing the touch.

His touch.

A bolt of longing shot through him, causing him to catch his breath.

What is happening?

And yet, he felt sure he knew exactly what was happening. Like him, she was out of practice being so close to someone;

a man in her case, a woman in his. She felt the energy of his touch, the warmth, and something inside her wanted to capture it within this moment that had broken through the typical boundaries and set all the protocols aside.

He found himself very much wanting to be caught.

There was a dreamlike quality to this encounter that seemed to blend what was acceptable and what was fantastical as he rubbed his thumb against her uninjured cheek. She made a sound almost like a kitten's purr that moved through him like a hunger. Her hand still holding his wrist tightened, and he leaned in as though drawn by an invisible force, then stopped. This was madness! Kenneth Bartholomew Winterton, heir presumptive to the Earl of Brenston did not kiss strange women on the side of the road!

She lifted her chin toward him. Anticipating. Bringing her face closer to his.

As a final grasp for propriety, he reminded himself of what Uncle Lester had said so often: everything he did was a reflection on his position. Kenneth was the heir to an earldom now. He was a man of power and position, and his behavior needed to reflect the values of the whole.

But he was also a man who had not felt what he was feeling for so long that he sometimes wondered if he would ever feel it again.

Blood warm in his veins.

A quickening of his breath.

The unseen pull drawing him to a woman who was feeling the exact same thing.

Her eyes were still closed when he pressed his lips to hers. She startled, but then wrapped her free hand around his other wrist and yielded completely while not letting him remove his hands from her face. This woman was hungry.

As hungry as he was.

The combination of their wanting was intoxicating, and as he deepened the kiss, she met him passion for passion. Want for want.

He pulled back from the kiss after several seconds, taking a deep breath in order to recenter himself to time and place. The gentlemanly thing to do would be to apologize for taking a liberty, but he was not sorry.

When her eyes fluttered open and a smile graced her lips, he felt sure she was not sorry either.

"Who are you?" she asked in a low whisper.

He opened his mouth to tell her his name and then stopped. Who was he?

Chapter Four

Who was that man? Rebecca asked herself as she walked beside Rose and mentally reviewed what had happened. She knew his name, of course, Malcolm Henry, and that he was the valet for the new heir to the earldom—but what sort of man kissed a woman the way he had kissed her after knowing her for only minutes?

What kind of woman grabbed hold of him so that he would not stop?

Was it a common practice for him?

If she encountered him again, would he kiss her again?

"Are you sure you're alright, Mama?"

Rebecca turned to her daughter walking alongside her and smiled a bit wider to hide her thoughts. "I am fine," she assured her, pulling back her shoulders and patting Rose's arm. "A bit shaken, but no worse for wear."

She had kissed a man—a *stranger*—on the side of the road

on a beautiful sunny day. And she felt more alive than she had in years. The still-damp handkerchief was in her reticule.

Rose's eyebrows remained furrowed, though Rebecca tried not to notice as they walked arm in arm toward town. "You are lucky you did not break a bone."

Rebecca was confused by the idea of a kiss so intense it could break bones, then she realized Rose was referring to Rebecca's jump into the brambles along the roadside. Because, of course, Rebecca had said nothing of the kiss to her daughter. She'd only told the first part of the story to explain her torn dress, scraped cheek, and slight limp. Her ankle was tender when she put weight on it, but she could tell it wasn't serious.

Truth be told, she'd do it again if it would end the same way. What a wanton woman she was, and yet she felt little shame. To have a man touch her with such gentleness, to care over her welfare—especially since the injury had been his fault—to kiss her because he wanted to. She could feel no shame for that. No, she would hold to it tightly and let herself remember the sensation when the darker bits of life began pushing in.

"Mama?"

Rebecca came back to the present—again—and leaned into Rose's shoulder. "I am fine, I assure you. In fact, I think it is good for my blood to pump a bit stronger than it is used to from time to time. I will get an ointment for my scratch, and the dress will be easy enough to repair. But how are you? How is the baroness?"

"She is wonderful," Rose said with genuine delight as she instantly recovered from her concern. "I am helping with the preparations for the Mabon Ball in September." She squared her shoulders with pride.

"Really?" Mabon was the autumn equinox, when the day and night were of the exact same length. "The baroness hasn't held it since the baron's death. I am surprised she would do so now."

"She was undecided until a few weeks ago," Rose explained. "Then she announced she wanted to resurrect the tradition. Did you know it marks the baron and baroness's wedding anniversary?" she shrugged, and smiled, which showed how excited she was. "I think she has been missing him of late. She could plan the whole thing in a single afternoon if she chose to, but I think she prefers to have someone to discuss ideas with, which is why she's asked me to help. You would not believe the effort that goes into hosting such an event."

"It's very exciting that she would trust you to be involved. That is a great credit to you, Rose, and a remarkable opportunity."

Rose grinned and lifted her shoulders to her ears like a little girl, giddy with excitement. "We are also reading Shakespeare, and she is explaining all the parts that do not make sense to me, which is a great deal, I'm afraid. She is such an educated woman."

Rebecca swallowed her jealousy of a woman who could give Rose what she herself could not. She had wanted this for Rose, and had, in fact, championed this course for a long time, teaching Rose manners above her station and using her connections at Grangeford to encourage the possibility.

It had been an accomplishment on both their parts when Rose had interviewed for the position of the baroness's companion. Rebecca had celebrated with Rose when they were informed that she'd been hired, and then cried herself to sleep for two weeks after Rose had left for Grangeford.

Every child leaves their mother at some point, and at least Rose was still in Wakefield and working in a respectable household. They saw one another every week, and Rebecca knew she'd done right by her daughter. She could never regret that, but she missed her terribly. It had been an ache in her chest for months now.

"What are you reading with her right now?" Rebecca asked.

"A play called *The Two Gentlemen of Verona*. It is not one of his more popular pieces, as I understand it, and often dismissed as simple, but the story is really quite fascinating . . ."

They enjoyed nearly an hour together, walking through the village, talking with acquaintances they encountered along the way, and stopping at the apothecary for an ointment to treat Rebecca's scratch. They parted ways at the cathedral, and Rose turned back the way she had come while Rebecca continued toward home, letting her mind wander back to her afternoon encounter.

That kiss.

Rebecca knew all about the heir, of course. When Edward Brenston had died, the village had balanced their mourning with speculation about who would take his place. Rebecca had given the gossip as much attention as any other interesting detail that filtered around a village like Wakefield, but since the heir to the Brenston title would have little effect on her day-to-day life, she had not wondered over it too much. Daily life required a good deal of attention, and she did not have the time to invest in the comings and goings of the local nobility. She'd have never imagined, for instance, that this new heir would bring someone like Mr. Henry into her sphere.

Was he in her sphere?

She blushed at her arrogance. For all she knew, Mr. Henry kissed every woman he ran off the road. Perhaps, in fact, his kiss was nothing more than an apology for his brute of a horse.

But she'd felt something from him. A shared experience. A shared need for something pleasurable, yet innocent. She'd felt, in the moment his lips touched hers, that he was not only giving her something, but taking something for himself as well. Comfort. Connection. Filling a need, just as she was when she responded to such an unbelievable action.

Rebecca reached Father's house, the third in a row of seven, and the pleasant memory of the kiss faded away as the oh-so-familiar tension replaced every other thought and emotion. This was not a happy home; it had not been happy when she had been a child, and it had not improved in all the years since. But it was her place in the world for now, and she made the best of it. Every day.

She pushed all other thoughts aside and focused on the responsibilities waiting on the other side of the door. There were two bust silhouettes to finish before next week and a sitting to prepare for on Thursday.

Mr. Timoltson would be joining them for dinner tomorrow

night, which meant she would need to go to the butcher in the morning for a roast and make fresh bread in the afternoon. It would be the second time he'd come for dinner, and she suspected he would ask permission to officially court her soon. Until today, she'd assumed she would accept the proposal, if it came, because a woman of her age and in her position could not be too particular regarding her suitors. Marriage would free her from Father's home, and perhaps they could work together better if she did not live under his roof.

It was ridiculous to think that Mr. Henry would interfere with that plan, and yet, until today, Rebecca had accepted the idea of a cordial marriage as the best arrangement she could hope for—all that she could expect.

Her heart had broken into a thousand shards when David had died, and she never expected she could love again. She had not *wanted* to feel anything more than duty and gratitude should she remarry. But she'd felt something different today.

She'd felt warm.

Wanted.

Wanting.

Which meant it was possible for her to feel such things that she thought were solidly planted only in her past.

Which meant settling for a loveless marriage of duty and gratitude might not be her destiny. It was an overwhelming thought.

And, perhaps, salvation.

Chapter Five

The monstrous horse had delivered Kenneth to the stone wall much earlier than anticipated, which was not at all surprising given the horse's speed and energy. The early arrival gave Kenneth a great deal of time to wait under the cover of some trees. He spent the time reviewing that kiss over and over in his mind.

Her name was Rebecca Parker. A widow. A common woman by any standard, except that she kissed like . . . He could not think of an adequate metaphor. A woman drowning? A woman pleading for her life? Both were such severe comparisons. No, she simply kissed him like a woman who wanted to kiss a man. Easy. Pure. Invigorating.

It was a relief when he saw his carriage finally turn the bend and come to a stop. Part of him had feared he'd arrived at the wrong stone wall by the wrong church. He kept his chin down so the driver would not recognize him as he tied the rented horse to the back of the carriage.

Once inside, he sat across from Malcolm, who grinned sleepily, then stretched his arms before removing the greatcoat from his shoulders.

"I hope your ride was as lovely as my nap," Malcolm said, folding the coat over his arm. "I could get used to a gentleman's life. There is much to be envied."

Kenneth took the coat that Malcolm handed to him but made no move to remove his own jacket or hat. He was still thinking of those green eyes as he stared without focus at the window of the carriage. Those soft lips. The grip of her hands on his wrists to make sure he did not pull away.

Malcolm cleared his throat, drawing Kenneth's gaze to him. "I said, if you will please pay attention, that I hope your ride was as lovely as my nap and that I could get used to living life as a gentleman."

Malcolm raised his eyebrows, clearly expecting a reply, but Kenneth had heard no question in what he'd said. In fact, his valet's words didn't make any sense at all.

"I kissed a woman on the roadside, half a mile or so back," Kenneth said, the words tumbling out like candy from a bag. He pointed his thumb over his shoulder in the general direction of where he'd parted ways with Rebecca, who had told him after that first kiss she was meeting her daughter soon.

"Then I kissed her again," he said, as though he'd spoken the middle section of the story out loud, which he hadn't. "Two times! I kissed a woman I have never met *twice* in the span of five minutes after nearly running her down with the menace of a horse you chose for me, and she kissed me back and it was . . . remarkable." Invigorating. Awakening. Fun.

He leaned back against the cushions and felt his whole body relax now that he had validated the experience by explaining it. His muscles ached from the ride, and his feet hurt from the slightly-too-small boots, and yet he felt like he could run the rest of the way to Brenning Hall due to the energy coursing through him. After a few seconds, he looked up to see a surprised expression on Malcolm's face and furrowed his eyebrows.

"What is wrong?"

"I am going to need you to start at the beginning of this story and speak slowly so that I can make some sort of sense of it. You kissed a woman you have never met before? If you wanted Lord Brenston to despise you, it would have been far more convenient to offend him before you rented out your estate and moved two hundred and thirty miles north."

"I did not kiss her as myself, of course, but rather as, well, you."

Malcolm blinked. "Me?"

"Well, your name, but the rest of it was all me and all her. Truly, Malcolm, it was a kiss for the ages."

The corner of his own beaver-skin hat caught him just below his right eye. Malcolm had thrown it far harder than was necessary to get it from one side of the carriage to another.

"Ow," Kenneth exclaimed, bending over to pick up the hat from the carriage floor. He rubbed the spot below his eye. "What was that for?"

"Is that why you want to pretend to be me? So you can take advantage of women on roadsides, and I am the man who looks the part of a scoundrel?"

"What? No!" Kenneth defended. "It just . . . happened. I had no intention of kissing her, but then it was . . . It was just so very right."

Malcolm threw one boot at Kenneth's head and then the other.

Chapter Six

Rebecca had meant to change out of her walking shoes before dinner, but Father had gone into a rant right after she'd come home, and it had taken far too much time to calm him, which had put the rest of her day so far behind schedule that she'd not had the chance to change her shoes before Mr. Timoltson had arrived.

Father had been ornery all evening, complaining during dinner about how offended he still was by Lady Beth's refusal to bring her daughters to the studio. When Rebecca had interrupted his story to suggest that it was perhaps both unprofessional and unwise to complain against one of the most elevated women in the county, Father had left for the pub in a huff.

Rebecca and Mr. Timoltson had finished the dinner awkwardly, then she suggested they visit in the parlor after she changed her shoes. She had been uncomfortable all evening in her laced walking boots that clunked upon the floorboards.

Now, with her soft house slippers on, she stood in the parlor doorway and watched Mr. Timoltson. The invigoration she'd felt after yesterday's roadside kiss had left her feeling bold, curious, and a bit reckless.

Mr. Timoltson was tall and thin with graying hair and a long face. His mustache gave him a distinguished look, and the long sideburns supported his overall militant air, though he had never served. He was a clerk by trade, quiet, respectable, and relatively dull.

Rebecca had believed the lack of attraction she felt toward Mr. Timoltson was because she could not feel such things for anyone after David's death. After yesterday's kiss with Mr. Henry, however, she was thinking differently. She *could* feel attraction and invigoration, and though she had initially thought the change was because of Mr. Henry specifically, she'd begun to wonder if it had nothing to do with him after all.

What if, instead, she had reached some internal point of healing where such feelings were possible? The feelings could have shown themselves on a roadside encounter with a stranger simply because her defenses were down, and she was not thinking about her incapability.

Something about Mr. Henry's proximity and his caring actions had broken her open yesterday afternoon. She'd wanted to be kissed, and he'd known it. But was the change of feeling because of the man or the circumstances? She had taken quite a tumble when she'd jumped out of the way of that beastly horse; perhaps she'd hit her head.

It was time for an experiment.

She took a breath, put a smile on her face, and entered the room.

"I apologize for my father's behavior at dinner, Mr. Timoltson," she said, causing him to turn toward her from where he'd been perusing the bookshelves. "He has had a difficult day and, I'm afraid, attempted to remedy it with more wine than was wise."

"Of course, Mrs. Parker," he said, nodding slightly, his arms clasped behind his back. "Do not fret on my account."

She joined him in front of the bookshelves and stood closer than she normally would, their arms nearly touching. Did she feel anything? Was there an increase of energy between them because they were so close to one another, or was she simply feeling the anxiety of her forward behavior?

"Do you enjoy reading, Mr. Timoltson?"

"I do," he said. "History mostly."

They stood in silence for several seconds while Rebecca waited for him to say something else. When he didn't, she reached in front of him to pull a volume from the shelves, allowing her arm to brush against his. She lifted the book and turned so she was standing directly in front of him, close enough to smell his aftershave and the pipe tobacco on his coat.

"Have you read this? *Lives of the British Admirals* by Alexander Donaldson?" It was not a very romantic title, but she simply needed a book. Any book.

He looked into her eyes, his cheeks slightly flushed. "I have not," he said.

Fortune favors the bold, she told herself. She lifted her chin invitingly as she held the book to her chest. "Perhaps we could read it together."

She took a small step forward, until there were only inches separating them—creating a similar proximity as she'd had with Mr. Henry. Did she feel invigorated? Was the air changed between them? Or was she just feeling extremely uncomfortable?

Mr. Timoltson swallowed.

She smiled and cocked her head to the side in what she hoped was a coy manner.

He stood stock-still.

She waited.

And waited.

"Kiss me," she finally whispered.

His face flushed scarlet. "What?"

"Kiss me, Mr. Timoltson."

He kept staring, and she felt her annoyance and embarrassment growing in equal measure. She very much wanted to be favored by the boldness, not humiliated.

She took a breath and made one more attempt. "I have appreciated your attention these last weeks, Mr. Timoltson, and understand your intention. We are not children, so let us not waste time pretending this is anything other than what it is—the chance for us to spend time together so we might know if we would make a good match. Kiss me, please, as part of that process."

He swallowed.

Then he kissed her.

She felt nothing.

When Rebecca closed the front door behind him a few minutes later, she leaned her forehead against the wood and thought about Mr. Henry. The sensations he'd drawn from her. The shared wanting of the exchange.

Maybe she hadn't felt the same with Mr. Timoltson because she'd planned it. Maybe his nervousness prevented it. Perhaps it would take repeated attempts before they shared the same feelings she'd shared with Mr. Henry.

Her motivation to pursue that possibility with Mr. Timoltson was decidedly low, however. If she had additional men to use as continued experiments, perhaps she would kiss them all and weigh the evidence, but a woman of virtue did not behave that way. She *was* a woman of virtue—kissing a stranger on the roadside notwithstanding—to say nothing of kissing two men in two days.

She felt her cheeks flush with heat, but, just as she'd considered yesterday, felt no shame. Life had become a dull existence these last months since Rose had left, and after meeting Mr. Henry, she was envisioning brighter possibilities for herself. How could she feel bad about that?

She had not heard from Mr. Henry. It would not be hard for him to find her if he wanted to, which meant he likely didn't want to, but then it had been only one day. It would not be wise to pin her hopes on him. And yet, it would be helpful to see him again, if only to see if it felt as invigorating to be around him a second time. She would not kiss him, of course, just be in his presence.

Besides, she still had his handkerchief, and it would be wrong to keep his property, wouldn't it?

Chapter Seven

T hat is the next step," Uncle Lester said after outlining his plans for the fields come spring.

Kenneth was used to managing a far smaller parcel of land. To consider acres and acres of land used in multiple aspects of agriculture made his head spin. But it was also exciting to stretch the boundaries of his former experience. He always enjoyed learning.

"Have you any questions?" Uncle Lester asked as he leaned back in his chair on the other side of the mahogany desk.

"No," Kenneth said.

He was careful to hide the notes he'd taken regarding the different agreements his uncle had in place with other gentry who used his lands, primarily for grazing. Uncle Lester would not approve of the doodles and designs that graced every page, but Kenneth concentrated better when he was drawing.

Kenneth would like more than handshakes to secure the

arrangements, especially since the handshake agreements had not included *his* hand, but there would be time to secure those things. Though Uncle Lester was nearing seventy years of age, he was in good health, and his mind was sharp.

"There is one more matter I would like to discuss as part of today's review," Uncle Lester said, interlacing his fingers and resting them on his ample belly that strained against the buttons of his waistcoat.

Kenneth raised his eyebrows expectantly.

"Lady Beth."

Kenneth's stomach dropped, but he kept his expression neutral. He'd been fearing this topic since his arrival. Lady Beth was a few years younger than Kenneth and was well established in both Brenning Hall and the Wakefield community.

"She is a good daughter and has given me three lovely granddaughters who have enlivened my life greatly these last years. I want to see her cared for in the manner she is used to after I am gone, and I am counting on you to make that possible. I would like you to—"

"No, my lord," Kenneth said, unwilling to hear the rest of the sentence, that was how opposed he was to this line of conversation.

"No, what?"

"I will not marry Lady Beth."

The old man bolted upright in his chair, sputtering, as his face turned red. "M-marry my daughter! What? Have you designs on *my daughter*!" He gripped the armrests of his chair, and he looked as if he might launch himself forward at any moment and tackle Kenneth to the ground.

Kenneth lifted his hands, palms out to defend himself. "No, I assure you I do not have any designs, but I thought you were asking me to—"

"I am asking you to make sure she is cared for," Uncle Lester cut in, spitting slightly as he spoke. "Act as trustee over the security I have arranged for her."

The room fell completely silent save for Kenneth's heart thundering in his chest. "Of . . . of course. I am sorry for assuming."

Uncle Lester eyed him suspiciously as he leaned back in his chair. "As you should be," he said in a tone of disgust. "The very idea . . ." He stopped and took a breath. "You are cousins!"

"But amid the noble classes that is not unheard of," Kenneth started, trying to defend his assumption, his face on fire, though he doubted it could be any redder than Uncle Lester's.

"In my household it is!"

"I am sorry, my lord, please forgive me."

Several seconds passed, during which Uncle Lester's face almost returned to its normal complexion.

Almost.

Kenneth wanted to curl into a ball and roll away, down the stairs, and out the front door. He was imagining himself rolling clear across the country when Uncle Lester spoke again.

"I am having repairs made on the dowager's cottage, which is located on the south end of the property. I have rented it for some years to my solicitor's mother, but she passed last summer, and so it is ready to be refurbished. I shall be adding some rooms, of course, to accommodate the girls while they are yet unmarried, but I want your assurance that Lady Beth will be welcome there, as will my granddaughters, indefinitely. As it is part of the entailment, I cannot demand such accommodation but am requesting your assurance all the same."

Kenneth squirmed again. This was an uncomfortable topic without him having jumped to such embarrassing conclusions. He'd managed to complicate the complications.

As further proof of this ability, his mind recalled the woman he'd kissed on the side of the road last week, but he pushed the memory away. Not because it was unwelcome, but this was not the time. He needed to focus.

"I feel very uncomfortable staying here in Brenning Hall while the family who has lived and loved here for so long moves to other accommodations. I would feel much more comfortable taking the dowager cottage and allowing Lady Beth and her daughters to stay on at Brenning Hall."

Uncle Lester shook his head, his fleshy jowls jiggling. "That would never do. You shall be Lord Brenston at that point, with a wife of your own ready to step into the role of countess. Your place is here."

"But it is their home," Kenneth said.

"Because I am Lord Brenston, and Lady Beth is my daughter," Uncle Lester said, as though the matter were that simple. "I hold title and rank and that gives my daughter and granddaughters the privilege to utilize this house and all its accommodation. When I am gone, they are entitled to the continued benefits of that association, but they cannot displace your position. Suggesting that you take the cottage is an entirely inappropriate thought, and one of the many ways in which you continue to show your lack of awareness for the protocols of your position."

He paused for a breath, his irritation rising. "You will be an *earl*, Kenneth, and you must respect that position if you expect anyone else to. You are to be a pillar of this community; it is your due to receive the deference and accommodation of that rank. You need to think like a nobleman, and when you show your limitations toward that understanding, it causes me a *great* deal of discomfort."

Kenneth swallowed and looked at the top of the desk. "I am sorry for causing you discomfort, Uncle. That is the last thing I want to do."

"Then listen to what I am telling you. And look me in the eye!"

Kenneth raised his head and met the old man's eye.

Uncle Lester's lips were tight. "You have to dispose of your own opinions, Kenneth, your way of thinking. You are no longer Kenneth Winterton, a gentleman with limited fortune. You will be an earl. A peer of the realm. A trusted member of court and community. The title precedes you into every room, every relationship, every decision. You do not think what is best for any individual—not even yourself—but what is best for the community affected by your status. Nothing comes above that responsibility. Nothing at all."

Not even Lady Beth, apparently. Kenneth would stay in this huge fortress, and Lady Beth would move into an eight-room house roughly the size of the ballroom at Brenning Hall. Her daughters would leave the luxury they had known, and their rooms here would lay empty. It felt immoral, and yet this was apparently the morality that the class structure of Great Britain depended upon.

Kenneth was trying so hard to live by his uncle's standards and felt renewed frustration at having disappointed him again. He'd truly thought he'd come to a good solution.

"Do you understand me?" Uncle Lester demanded.

"Yes, my lord, I understand." *But I do not like it, and I do not know if I shall ever be the man you want me to become.*

During the next hour, they reviewed the details of Lady Beth's situation and the accommodations Lord Brenston had made for her. He had been very generous, and Kenneth agreed to every stipulation. It was a relief when Uncle Lester changed the subject until he realized what the new topic was to be.

"I have invited two local families to dinner tomorrow night: the Harrops, and Mr. Jude Wright and his daughter, Elizabeth. She is twenty-four years of age, a bit of a bluestocking, but well connected. It is time for you to find a wife."

"So, the hunt is to begin?" The audience was not a good fit for the attempted levity.

"The hunt began the day you became my heir," Uncle Lester said, glaring. "But as of tomorrow, you will have been here for a week. I expect you to be married before Christmas."

Kenneth managed a nod, but his stomach felt tight with anxiety as he was dismissed. He'd planned to go for a ride—the nice, leisurely sort that Uncle Lester approved of—but now wanted nothing more than to fall face down on his bed and take a nap. He never napped.

But then, he'd never sat across a desk discussing another man's death for hours, or the fact that he was expected to pick a wife from a crowd much as he might choose a potato from a pile. Would he ever feel comfortable in his new place in the world?

Could he fill this role?

Uncle Lester never ducked his head when he was introduced as Lord Brenston. He took his place at the head of the table without question, he spoke over anyone beneath him without hesitation, and he saw himself as set apart to take his place as a leader. Edward had possessed the same confidence since the time he was a boy. Kenneth feared he would always feel like an ordinary man in an extraordinary position.

He walked to the window at the end of the hall and looked upon the lands that would one day be his. They stretched for miles. One day, he would be the one responsible for managing every bit of it.

To the south was the village of Wakefield; he could see the cathedral spires above the trees and the roofs of some of the buildings. To the north, he could see the gray stone of Grangeford, where the Baroness Konold lived. Their properties bordered one another, though there were hundreds of acres between the estate houses themselves.

Kenneth had been told that her son, Baron Konold, had been scampering about India for the last decade while she managed his holdings in his place. Kenneth wished someone else could do his work here for him. Not that he wanted to scamper across the world, but the thought that he would remain here, learning to live a life that was uncomfortable with a woman whom he did not know while waiting for an old man he loved to die, made him extremely sad.

"There you are."

Kenneth looked over his shoulder as Malcolm approached. He joined Kenneth at the window, then looked around the hall to make sure they were alone before pulling a letter from the inside of his coat.

"This was delivered through the kitchens this morning," he said, his voice low. "I quickly determined it was not actually meant for me." He quirked a half smile as he extended the letter to Kenneth.

Kenneth took the letter with trepidation until the pieces of the puzzle snapped together. There was only one person who would send a letter to his valet that was actually intended for him. He quickly unfolded the letter and scanned the words written in a decidedly feminine hand.

"Gracious," he whispered as he finished, his mouth staying open. "She wants to meet me. Where is Grover Park?"

"I have no idea," Malcolm said dryly. "But I'm assuming that you would like me to find out and that you are going to want my coat again even though this is a bad idea."

"It is a *terrible* idea," Kenneth agreed, striding quickly toward his tower room. He envisioned the woman in blue penning this note to him, and the tension of the meeting with Uncle Lester disappeared in the anticipation of seeing her again. "This world is full of them."

Chapter Eight

The longer Rebecca sat on the bench in Grover Park, the more she suspected she was being foolish. It was Mr. Henry's prerogative to call on her if he wanted to further their connection. Yet she was in possession of his personal property—a handkerchief she'd scrubbed clean, dried, and pressed into a perfect square.

It was right that she should return it.

But it was wrong to ask him to meet her.

But it was right for her to follow her curiosity now that it was piqued.

But it was wrong to have kissed him.

Except that it had not felt wrong at all.

Not. One. Little. Bit.

She did not take off her bonnet—there were other people at the park—but she did lift her face to the sun and push away her worries about having requested this meeting with Mr. Henry, about Father's increasingly poor disposition, and about what she would say to Mr. Timoltson the next time he called on her. She took a breath, enjoying the moment of sunshine, and tried to hold the moment tightly.

And she thought back to the kiss.

There had been a few very specific moments in Rebecca's life when she had known she was exactly where she was meant to be. One was when she had been twelve years old and her younger sister, Constance, had stumbled while they were crossing Broom's creek. Rebecca had known just where to go further down the creek to wade in and catch her. She hadn't been afraid; she'd known exactly what to do.

Another perfect moment was when she'd held Rose in her arms for the first time. It had been a grueling delivery over the course of two days, but when she'd held her red-faced, squalling daughter in her arms, she'd known that this was a moment she'd been created for.

Leaving church in the middle of services and arriving home in time to hold David's hand for his final breaths had been another instance.

There were less-dramatic examples: finding the perfect bolt of cloth with just enough to make the dress she'd envisioned, finding wild mushrooms the day before Easter, or visiting a friend on a day when the friend very much needed someone for support.

There was something about that kiss that felt similar, as though it was meant to happen, and that it was teaching her something, preparing her for something. It was important. Seeing Mr. Henry again would be important too.

Somehow, she just knew it.

Chapter Nine

The day was lovely, made even lovelier for the excitement coursing through Kenneth's veins. It made no sense for him to be this excited, and perhaps that was what he liked most—the senselessness of it. His life had become so specific these last months as he prepared to come to Wakefield, and this was fluid and . . . fun. Were earls allowed to have fun? Perhaps only when pretending *not* to be an earl.

You are not an earl yet, Kenneth reminded himself. Simple. Easy. Innocent. Fun. That is where he would keep his focus.

Grover Park was a large park on the east side of the village. Part of it was manicured and included a graveled walking path upon which strolled other visitors enjoying the summer day. At one point, the path diverged with one path looping back through the maintained grounds and around a small pond. The other direction of the path led into a wooded area where the gravel turned to packed earth as it wound into thick trees and dense shrubbery. Mrs. Parker had said she'd be waiting for him on that wooded path. He was dressed in a set of Malcolm's clothes but with an older pair of his own boots so his feet weren't pinched.

Mrs. Parker was sitting at a bench with her eyes closed, and her face lifted toward the sunlight filtering through the tree branches. She looked so relaxed that he hesitated to interrupt and, instead, took the time to study her face and figure and remember the energy of their kiss in full detail. When he could not wait any longer to make eye contact with her and enjoy her smile for no other reason than because she was happy to see him, he took a step forward.

The sound of his crunching footsteps must have alerted her. Her eyes blinked open, and she sat up straight. Their eyes met; she smiled and then stood.

He stopped a few feet away from her and resisted the desire to reach out his hand and touch her arm, her cheek, her hair. He wasn't sure how to greet her. Would a valet bow over her hand the way a gentleman bowed over the hand of a lady?

"You came," she said simply.

Hearing her voice softened his anxiety. "I did, Mrs. Parker."

"Please call me Rebecca," she said.

"Alright, Rebecca, but then you must call me . . . Malcolm." The hesitation felt like breaking the lead of his pencil. Discordant and disruptive to the scene before him.

She did not seem to notice his hesitation. Her smile widened, and they stared at one another for the space of several seconds before she looked away.

"Forgive me for the boldness of my invitation," Rebecca said, taking her reticule from her arm. "I wanted to return your handkerchief and was not sure how else to call on you."

He put out his hand to stop her from opening the bag. He did not want to have come all this way only to take his hand-kerchief and leave. He wanted time with her. Time away from everything else. "Can we walk first?"

She lifted her eyebrows. "You want to walk with me?"

"If you have the time."

She smiled, a beautiful wide smile he remembered from their first meeting, from when he'd pulled back from their kiss and known that not only had she wanted him to kiss her but that she had been glad he did.

"I have time to walk," she said.

"Wonderful," he said, putting out his arm while hoping that wasn't out of place. All classes walked arm in arm, didn't they? It wasn't simply a gentry action?

She looped her arm though his as though they had done it a hundred times, and he relaxed. He guided them toward the wilderness path, which offered some seclusion from the more open areas of the park, and she did not deter his course.

"You are not limping any longer," he said after a few steps.

"All was well after a good night's sleep."

"Let me see the scratch," he said, stopping and turning to face her as she did the same.

She turned her head to the left; the scratch was pink instead of red and showed no signs of inflammation. He lifted his hand and traced his thumb just below the scratch. She closed her eyes, and he felt the sensations coursing through him, drawing his energy toward hers. This time, however, he took charge instead of acting on the feelings sparking in his belly.

They were not alone in the park.

He dropped his hand and waited for her to open her eyes before he spoke. "It seems to be healing well."

"Yes."

They held each other's eyes a moment longer, then he turned forward and led them back to walking. This was dangerous—them being so alone. But it was also wonderful to not feel as though he were being watched, evaluated, and measured. He felt the ease settle into his muscles and bones.

"How long have you served as Mr. Winterton's valet?"

Hearing his name on her lips in the wrong context spurred his anxiety, and it took a few moments for him to remember both who he was and who he was supposed to be. The realization undermined the ease. He was a liar. This woman, who made him feel more like himself than anyone else, was the victim of his lies. Yet he could not change it. *Would* not change it. For both their sakes. He knew Malcolm's history well enough to recite it, which would prolong their time together. If she knew who he truly was, she would not be here.

"We actually served together in the navy several years ago. When circumstances required his need of a valet, he offered me the position."

She lifted her eyebrows. "He asked you to give up your situation?"

Kenneth's cheeks flushed. That wasn't how it had felt to

Malcolm, was it? "Well, I am a tailor's son, so I know clothing, and I had been working as a footman in a household in Dursley. It was an improvement of my circumstances."

"So, you had not been a valet before?"

"No." The word was clunky on his tongue, and he wished he knew how to speak of something else, but talking about their past and their present was how people got to know one another. He felt like a heel.

Rebecca smiled. "And you are happy with the work?"

"Yes." He was feeling extremely uncomfortable.

"I was in service for a time," Rebecca said. "A chambermaid at Grangeford."

She'd been in service? That widened the gap between them even more, but he answered so as not to create an awkward break in the conversation. "That is Lord Konold's estate?"

"Yes, the Baroness Konold, as she prefers to be called rather than Lady Konold, is in residence for now. Lord Konold, her son, is abroad."

"I have heard of her," Kenneth said, though he wasn't certain Malcolm actually had.

"My daughter, Rose, has been her companion these last four months. It's been a wonderful opportunity for her."

She had been in service, and now her daughter was? "How long ago were *you* employed by the household?"

"Oh, goodness, nearly twenty years ago now. Before my daughter was born."

She went on to talk about her late husband, David, who had been a successful enough brick mason that she had not had to continue in service after Rose's birth. "I work with my father now and keep house for him. It has been a good life."

A good life. He liked that she'd said that. He'd always believed that people who were generally happy with their past had a better chance of being happy with their present.

"What about you?" she asked. "Do you like the work of a valet more than that of a footman?"

Kenneth hesitated. It was uncomfortable to share facts about Malcolm's life, but more uncomfortable still to share Malcolm's opinions. *Did* Malcolm like the work?

Kenneth thought instead of his own efforts of learning how to become a man of rank. "I am grateful for it," he said, honestly. "It is an excellent opportunity for both me and my sons."

"Yes, but do you *like* it?"

He took another breath, lining up the words that were true. "It was unexpected, and so I do not feel adequately . . . trained, but I am learning, and I am determined to do well. Be worthy of the post."

"Worthy?" she said, turning to look at him. "I hope you are not basing your worth on your position."

He felt her words deeply. They looked at one another in silence, making him realize they'd stopped walking. "I am trying not to."

"Your post is something designed by man for the governing of our lives here. It does not determine your value or worth in the sight of God or the people who truly matter."

"I-I have never thought of it that way."

She shrugged as though she had not said something monumental. "You mentioned you have sons—how many?"

Malcolm did not have sons. Kenneth's stomach sank further as he was put in the same twisted spot he'd been before.

"I only have one daughter, Rose," Rebecca said before he could answer. "I miss her terribly."

"I miss my boys as well." Both boys would be coming to Brenning Hall for Christmas, but Kenneth could not tell her that. He also could not talk to her about Christopher's schooling or Jeremy's summer visit to a friend's estate in Brighton. A valet's sons would never be able to pursue such courses.

They walked for nearly half an hour, speaking of his sons as much as he dared and her daughter; his situation and hers. Except it wasn't his situation. The line between truth and lie became less and less clear the more they spoke, and he became increasingly aware of the horror of his actions. Rebecca listened to every word, believing the tale he was spinning. Several times he thought to tell her the truth, but imagining how she would feel drove the idea off, until some new point rose up and reminded him of how unsustainable this was.

She would eventually learn who he was—he was not fool enough to believe otherwise—and the more he played this out, the more it would hurt her. And yet, even amid the untruths, he was speaking more freely of his feelings than he had to anyone else. She listened and asked questions and genuinely seemed to care. It made the deception even worse, and yet all the more intoxicating.

She'd shared with him as well, about her father's work—he

was an artist—and her own struggle with adapting to a life she did not expect after her husband's death. He sensed a similar fatigue in her tale that she was not well versed in telling. There was something here between them, a trust, a connection.

A complete impossibility.

The trail came out of the trees, and they stopped walking at the same time, as though realizing that whatever dream they'd been in had come to an end. She turned to him, and he met her bright green eyes.

"The path has never been so short," she said.

"Perhaps because the company has never been so good," he said, then heard the possible interpretation of his words and tried to amend them. "I mean, your company, of course, not mine. That would be very . . . arrogant."

"It was certainly because the company was so good," Rebecca said with a wide smile.

They held each other's eyes again for several seconds.

"I have your handkerchief," she finally said, breaking the spell and opening her reticule that had hung at her wrist throughout their walk.

She held out the cloth, washed and pressed into a perfect square.

He stared at it, remembering that day and the lie he'd told her about his identity. Multiple lies had now been added to the first one. She would return this handkerchief, and he would likely never see her again.

"Are you alright?" she asked after several seconds had passed, his handkerchief still in her hand.

"Rebecca," he said. "I owe you an apology. I—"

"Do not apologize," she said without a hint of humor in her voice even though she smiled as she said it. "And do not think I am asking anything from you, Malcolm. I am here to thank you, for . . . well, for everything. And to return your property."

Kenneth pulled his eyebrows together. Thank him? What did she mean by that?

She took hold of his wrist with one hand and pressed the handkerchief into his palm with the other, wrapping his fingers around the cloth and keeping her gloved hand wrapped around his. "Thank you, Malcolm."

She let go of his hand, then turned and left him standing there. She was twenty paces away before he ran to catch up with her. It was madness, but he could not let her leave without knowing he would see her again.

"Meet me again," he said, somewhat breathless.

She stopped and looked at him. "Really?"

He nodded, already excited by the prospect. "Next week, at the same time right here."

She smiled and nodded. "Alright, I'll meet you here again at the same time next week."

"I shall look forward to it," he said, grinning.

"As will I."

He watched until she turned down the path, out of sight. He was eager and excited and warmed all the way through by this madness he absolutely knew he would eventually regret.

Chapter Ten

Rebecca felt almost giddy as she made her way home. Malcolm had shared his feelings with her and listened to hers. It had been so easy to talk of things she did not normally talk about, certainly not with a man. She had women friends, and her sister, Constance, with whom she confided through letters since she lived in Bower, but this had been different. Putting her story into a narrative for someone who knew nothing of her had brought a different sort of clarity. It had helped her, perhaps, to see herself from a different perspective.

The part that stood out to her was that she had given up a great deal of hope when David had died; so much of her confidence and expectation had gone with him. She'd never imagined she'd be alone or that the life they'd spent years building would come to an end. The loss had made her shrink within herself and give up any hope that she could be happy again. That she *should* be happy again.

She'd moved into Father's house with Rose and made her daughter her focus. Returning to the house had meant accepting Father's meanness, stepping in to do his work, and doing everything she could to protect Rose from the worst of her father's temper.

Rose was now officially on her own path. Father's disposition was getting increasingly worse, making her time at the house increasingly uncomfortable. Yet she had not responded to Mr. Timoltson's invitation to have dinner with him and his children on Sunday night. She did not want to be with Mr. Timoltson when she knew that she could feel so much more.

She wanted to be with Malcolm, and the thought made her cheeks flush hot. Did she dare consider the possibility? The idea brought a flutter to her belly, so strong she pressed her hand upon the place. For some time, she'd been feeling the need to change her situation. How long could she wait to see what might become of this connection with Malcolm?

Rebecca helped at Grangeford when they needed extra servants for a dinner party now and again, and Mrs. Lenning, the housekeeper, had hinted that if Rebecca ever wanted a full-time position again, she need only ask. But Rebecca did not want to live in service if she did not have to. It was a step below what her life had become with David and even with her father. Marriage was the most obvious way out of Father's house, but it felt like a different sort of captivity if she did not feel the connection that she now knew was possible.

She *could* feel attraction.

She had life and love yet to give.

And he wanted to see her again.

Still wrapped in the fresh excitement of her thoughts, Rebecca opened the door to Father's studio and stepped over the threshold. She could hear nothing from the main level that housed the studio itself and a parlor for clients. She opened the door leading to the stairs and climbed them slowly toward the family level—kitchen, parlor, and study.

When she reached the kitchen, the scrape of a chair leg on the floor drew her attention toward the table. She looked in time to see the mug hurling through the air toward her. She ducked, covering her head and gasping as the pottery crashed into the lintel where it shattered. She felt a sharp pain in her shoulder and another just below her ear as she dropped into a crouch and lifted her hands to cover her face.

"Where have you been?" Father's voice bellowed so loudly she felt sure the walls were shaking. Or was it just her body shaking in response to what had just happened? If he'd hit her with that mug . . .

"There is a sitting at one o'clock," he continued. "And the studio has not been set!"

One o'clock? That was hours from now. Except she'd stayed at the park far longer than she'd expected. She lifted her head enough to look at the clock in the parlor. He was right. There was only half an hour until the sitting.

"I-I am sorry, Father. I lost track of time."

"You lost track of time?" he repeated with derision.

She felt warm blood trailing from the cut beneath her ear, and the physical sensation brought more clarity to the situation.

He'd thrown a piece of crockery at her! The only reason he'd missed hitting her directly was because she'd managed to duck in time.

Rebecca forced herself to stand up straight, though her legs trembled, and she had to put one hand on the wall to keep her balance. She put her other hand to the stinging at her neck and pulled her fingers away, blood on the tips, which made her shake even more. She looked from her fingers to her father, whose eyes were still red and angry, who showed no concern for the injury he'd caused—never mind the injury he could have caused. He had never been kind, but this was something new, something frightening, and she felt a surge of self-protection rise up within her.

Honor thy father and thy mother.

Spare the rod and spoil the child.

I will make a way in the wilderness and rivers in the desert.

"I am going for my constitutional," Father said. "I expect all to be in readiness when I return." He said nothing more as he exited the room, clomping down the stairs and slamming the door behind him.

Rebecca made her way to the basin where she wet a cloth and held it to the cut on her neck, her whole body shaking as hot tears ran down her face.

She was not safe here, and waiting for things to change was no longer an option.

Chapter Eleven

"And what do you think of our valley?" the baroness asked, her sharp eyes never leaving Kenneth's face. This was not the first interrogation he had sat through since coming to Wakefield, nor was she the most fearsome of the morning callers he'd sat across from these last weeks, but she had a presence that demanded he not take her lightly. Being aware of the connection she afforded to Rebecca through Rose, who was employed by the elegant woman, put him on edge. It was a connection he could not reference because he was an idiot who was playing out a losing hand.

Focus!

"It is lovely," Kenneth said, "but of course you know that. I understand you have lived in Wakefield all your life."

She went on to recount her history, much of which Uncle Lester had briefed Kenneth on that morning in preparation of the visit. She filled in the details of having been a merchant's daughter, then a baron's wife, and now a baron's mother.

Kenneth opened his mouth to ask about her having been a merchant's daughter, but Lady Beth cut in before he could speak.

"The baroness manages her son's holdings in his place," Lady Beth added.

"Is that so?" Kenneth said, though he was already aware. A key point of small talk was simply to ask questions—even if you knew the answer—in order to keep the conversation going. "That is quite a feat."

"Well, I have been mistress of the home for nearly fifty years," the baroness said, lightly tapping her cane on the floor, her smile showing how pleased she was with her accomplishment. "I daresay I am the most qualified."

Lady Beth laughed as though the baroness had made a joke.

Kenneth glanced at her, embarrassed by his cousin's misinterpretation, then met the baroness's eye. The baroness was still smiling as she rolled her eyes toward the ceiling for only a moment as Lady Beth turned to pick up her teacup. Kenneth pinched his lips together to keep from smiling too broadly.

Rebecca had called the baroness a remarkable woman. Kenneth was beginning to understand why. She owned her place in the polite world—it had entered the room with her—but she seemed to have a broader perspective than some of the other noble class.

"I hope one day to feel the similar connection to this land and these people that you feel, Baroness," Kenneth said.

"You will," she said with a nod as she raised her cup of tea to her lips. "Your grandfather was the earl; it is in your blood. And you have a solid head upon your shoulders to make up for whatever the bloodline does not pass on."

They had only just met, but he sensed she was not making an idle remark.

A tap at the door drew the attention of all three of them.

"I am sorry to interrupt, my lady," Remmings, the butler, said, directing his comments to Lady Beth. "But Miss Gertney needs a word."

Miss Gertney was the music teacher who came in three days a week to school the girls in piano and harpsichord. The music room was located near the doorway that connected Kenneth's tower room to the common area of the house, and sometimes Kenneth would listen outside the door when he passed by during their practices—the girls were very proficient.

"Please excuse me," Lady Beth said, then bustled from the room, leaving Kenneth and the baroness alone.

As soon as the door clicked shut, the baroness put down her cup, and her gaze sharpened to a fine point upon him.

"Now, tell me, how has your transition been? From bachelor to family man must be a difficult adaptation—especially *this* family."

"They have been nothing but kind to me," Kenneth defended.

The baroness lifted one hand. "Oh, I do not mean to sound like a gossip. They are good people, and the girls are lovely, of course. I only mean that you have been your own man and now you are under obligation to the place. It is not an easy change, that is all."

"There are certainly more difficult hardships," Kenneth said, cautious in his response. He liked this woman, but he knew better than to trust her after so little time to know her.

Her smile fell. "I have handled this badly, haven't I? I've made you uncomfortable."

"Of course you haven't," Kenneth said because that was what he was expected to say. "I am glad to get the chance to know you."

The baroness was silent a few moments, then nodded. "Tell me about your sons," she said, changing the subject.

Kenneth was relieved, and readily obliged. "Christopher is at Oxford; he has two years left. And Jeremy will begin his studies in a few months. He is interested in being a professor of literature and is very much looking forward to University."

"Are you a student of literature?" she asked.

"Not as much as I would like to be," he admitted.

"What are your interests? Aside from estate management, of course."

He hesitated, feeling the desire to be more personal than he usually was. Perhaps it was because her interest was more sincere than he usually heard. "I find horsemanship very interesting," he said. "My father had quite a stock when I was younger."

She nodded but continued to look at him expectantly, as though she knew there was more.

"And . . . I like to draw." He had not revealed that detail to anyone since coming to Brenning Hall, but he felt compelled to satisfy her curiosity.

She lifted her eyebrows. "Really?" She sounded genuinely interested. "My husband considered himself an artist of sorts, though he preferred painting—watercolor mostly. Do you have anything you could show me?"

Kenneth straightened, his attention piqued. "Your husband was a painter?"

"Well," she said with a grin, "he was a baron who painted. It is an unusual talent for a man to pursue, but, well, the benefits of being a man of title is that you get the right to be a bit . . . eccentric. I think most people are happiest when they have a means of creation aside from business pursuits."

They spent a happy ten minutes discussing the late baron's artwork; several of his paintings apparently hung upon the walls at Grangeford. When Lady Beth rejoined them, the baroness smoothly shifted the conversation to other things, and the visit quickly came to an end.

Kenneth stood when the baroness did and bowed over her extended hand.

"I do hope you'll come and see my husband's work," the baroness said, smiling. "I would love to show you."

"I would like that," Kenneth said, excited by this connection.

"Perhaps your household would like to come to dinner next week. I can invite a few other people to join us so you can widen your circle of acquaintances. We have quite an extensive art collection at Grangeford, thanks to my husband. We are quite proud of it."

"Oh, that would be marvelous," Lady Beth said.

The baroness glanced at her and smiled, but immediately looked back at Kenneth, her eyebrows raised in a way that indicated to Kenneth that, though the invitation was for the family, it was primarily for him.

"I agree," Kenneth said. "That would be marvelous."

"Might you extend the invitation to include my Jacqueline, Baroness?" Lady Beth asked. "She is of an age for such things, and I would love for her to have as many opportunities to interact with society as possible before her season in London."

"I would love to have Miss Marlow in attendance," the baroness said.

"Thank you, Baroness. She will be so excited. I have heard you shall be holding the Mabon Ball again this year," Lady Beth continued.

"In fact, I am," the baroness said with a nod. "I have missed it."

Lady Beth turned toward Kenneth, her usually severe face looking more animated than he'd seen it. "The Mabon Ball is an event not to be rivaled in the county," she explained. "What a treat that you shall observe the grandeur of it, so soon after coming to Wakefield."

"All of your girls shall be invited, of course," the baroness said, then turned her attention toward Kenneth. "It is not so formal as events in Town, of course, but it does make for a lovely evening. Most of the county will be invited. I hope you will come."

"Of course, he shall," Lady Beth said. "Someone must serve as escort for Jacqueline."

Kenneth did not care all that much for dancing, and the idea of a party on such a grand scale as this one did not excite him, but he appreciated the baroness's invitation and would, of course, attend. It was his responsibility to find his place at such events. "Thank you, Baroness."

Upon the baroness's leaving, morning calls were finished, and Kenneth made his way to the stables where he would work with the new horse, bought from the posting inn where he'd hired it.

If he went to Grangeford, he might cross paths with Rose. The thought stopped him cold, and he stood in the hallway for several seconds as he considered that possibility. His usual discomfort had lifted for a moment during the baroness's visit but now returned in full force. Would he meet Rebecca's daughter when he went to Grangeford?

Would she look like her mother?

Would the dinner happen before or after he'd seen Rebecca again?

Chapter Twelve

As the second son of the fifth Earl of Brenston, Kenneth's father had inherited Cornercrest, a small estate in Sussex, and improved his situation primarily through breeding horses and sheep. Kenneth had not continued the horse husbandry, needing to take better advantage of the land, and had instead expanded the sheep herds and leased some of the land to mining, which had turned a better profit. He still enjoyed horsemanship, however, even if Uncle Lester felt that horses should be for transportation purposes only and not recreation.

The feisty horse Kenneth had rented from the posting inn had been a menace that day, but an intriguing one. It had one of the smoothest gaits Kenneth had ever experienced and unparalleled stamina. He'd managed to purchase it from the posting inn, and Uncle Lester had inspected the animal—as he inspected anything kept in his stables. Since the horse had been riderless during the inspection, Uncle Lester had seen a relatively docile horse with good lines and had approved Kenneth spending time working with the animal so long as it did not interfere with his responsibilities.

He'd also cautioned Kenneth about his behavior when he was riding in the country. "You are still my heir when you are not at Brenning Hall, and I expect you to conduct yourself in a way that will bring no embarrassment upon my house."

"Yes, Uncle," Kenneth had said that day nearly two weeks ago. But he had not meant it.

Uncle Lester disapproved of a great many things—elaborate knots in Kenneth's cravat, lace cuffs, boots that were anything less than high-polish, and Kenneth sitting on one side of a settee during visits instead of in his own chair.

Kenneth complied with most of his uncle's rules out of respect, but he could justify bending those rules for things his uncle would not see and therefore could not disapprove of.

His rebellion involved getting up early and dressing in a set of plain clothes, so that he looked the part of Malcolm and would be ignored by the grooms, and galloping through the countryside on his wild horse nearly every day. The rides were delightful and took the edge off his uncle's demands on his other time and manners.

After his morning rides, Kenneth would return to his tower room where Malcolm—who stayed out of sight while Kenneth was out—would be waiting to transform Kenneth into a gentleman again. Kenneth would breakfast with his uncle around nine, review whatever lesson they'd had the day before, and then spend the rest of the morning visiting with whoever came to call. If there was time, he would return to the stables as himself to do the necessary groundwork with Thunderbolt.

The horse's name had been Copper, even though it was bay-colored and far too extraordinary for such a common name. Kenneth had renamed the animal Thunderbolt, an apt description of what the horse became once there was a rider on his back. Working with the horse was as enjoyable as anything else he'd done since coming to Wakefield and something he looked forward to.

After his training time with Thunderbolt, Kenneth came inside for luncheon—today he dined with the Brenston granddaughters—and then made his way to his uncle's office for his daily lesson.

Today's focus of "How to be an earl" was on parliamentary duties, and Kenneth had a headache by the time they finished. He'd never had much interest in politics, but he would inherit a seat in the House of Lords one day and thus become a part of the making and enforcing of laws that would continue to build the country he loved. Edward had been taught these things every day of his life, whereas Kenneth had only a short time to absorb a lifetime of knowledge.

After the lesson, Kenneth went to his room in the tower and retrieved his sketch pad and pencil set, feeling the need to expend some energy in a creative pursuit. He perched himself on the window seat and sketched the view, which was extraordinary.

Being four stories up laid the Brenston lands out before him to the point where he could see the curvature of the horizon in the distance. As his pencil scratched upon the paper, he felt the tension within his chest begin to uncoil. At some point, he turned to fresh paper and began to sketch a different scene—Rebecca sitting on the bench in Grover Park with her eyes closed and her face toward the sun. It had been three days since they had met, and it would be four more before they met again.

Kenneth did not sketch people often—he mostly drew buildings and landscapes—but it was easy to bring Rebecca's features to mind. He tried to capture what it was that pulled him toward her, the *something* that had made such an impact upon him both times he'd been in her company. It was something beyond what his pencil could reveal, but he felt it when he looked upon the picture, appearing as though by magic on his paper.

There was no question of whether he could pursue her—he couldn't. She did not know who he was, while he knew exactly who she was. She would never be invited as a dinner guest to Brenning Hall. She would never be accepted in the circles Kenneth was expected to lead one day. She could not fill the role of countess or help anchor his place in the local society, which was the reason he needed a wife at all.

Perhaps most importantly, she would not be comfortable with a life she did not know. He had only to think of how uncomfortable it was for him to take *his* place even though he was only one generation removed from the title.

Rebecca would have none of that familiarity to build from—she'd been in service, for goodness' sake—which meant she would feel all he felt a hundredfold.

It is impossible.

So why had he made plans to see her again?

Why was he spending time sketching her and thinking about her?

Why did he allow himself to feel such excitement when it would only hurt them both?

He leaned back against the stone of the deep-set window and let out a breath as he looked across the lands that would one day be his. Grover Park was out there somewhere west of the cathedral spire towering above the trees.

He should cancel their meeting on Tuesday.

Seeing her again would mean he would have to perpetuate the lies he'd already told her, continue to craft this man who was a blend of Malcolm and himself—a man who did not exist. It wasn't right, and it was certainly unfair to her.

She trusts me.

The thought turned his stomach sour, and he set aside the sketch pad and scrubbed a hand over his face.

She trusts me even though I have lied to her each time we've met.

What if part of his interest was based upon the fact that she was out of reach? Did she represent a rebellion against the demands placed upon him, much like his rides on Thunderbolt each morning?

For her part, they were on equal ground and every possibility was before them. He'd supported that belief. He'd encouraged it. He'd *created* it.

Kenneth groaned and stood up to pace from one side to the other of his tower room. Each time he had seen her, he hurt her a little bit more.

He needed to cancel their meeting on Tuesday.

He did not want to.

There was a knock at the bedroom door—the wood was so thick he barely heard it—and a moment later, Malcolm opened the door.

"I was able to fix the seam," Malcolm said, holding a black dinner jacket.

He entered the room and placed the jacket on the edge of the bed. He began moving about to gather the different items of clothing Kenneth would be trussed into for tonight's dinner presentation to the crowds of onlookers.

"I learned a bit more about tonight's guests, as you requested," Malcolm said. "There are two unmarried women. Miss Huckstrom, who is twenty-six and has a failed engagement somewhere in her past—none of the staff knew the details—and Mrs. Trostle, who is in her forties, widowed two years ago. She'll have her oldest son with her; he is twenty-seven years of age, I believe.

"Mrs. Trostle is the one your uncle is particularly interested to have you meet, as Lord Brenston and her father were good friends in their youth, though they do not speak now after a situation involving some slippery sheep." He turned, a set of black evening trousers in one hand and a starched shirt front in the other, then furrowed his brow. "What is the matter?"

"Nothing," Kenneth said, retrieving his sketch pad from where he'd left it on the window seat. He looked at the sketch of Rebecca with her face to the sun before closing the book and shutting her away. "What could possibly be the matter with me when I have so much to be grateful for?"

"Well, you could have an upset stomach, a headache, or deep-seated regret over a certain misrepresentation of yourself as your valet." He shrugged as though each option were as trite as the other.

Kenneth was relieved Malcolm had brought up Rebecca. He wanted to talk about her all the time. "I am to see her again, Malcolm. And I know that I shouldn't."

"You are correct, you shouldn't." Malcolm began laying the articles on the edge of the bed in the order they would be put on. Then he stopped and regarded Kenneth. His tone held none of his usual amusement. "You *really* shouldn't see her again, Winterton. This has gone too far already."

"I know," Kenneth said, hearing the pathetic sadness in his tone. "I think I shall have to tell her the truth when we meet on Tuesday. She deserves that much at least." He sighed. "And then it shall be done."

Malcolm was silently respectful of the weight of those words. For seven seconds.

Malcolm clapped his hands and the jesting tone returned. "If you are lucky, she will scream at you instead of cry. Now, let us get to work. Your bride-to-be may very well sit across from you at the table tonight."

"You are not very kind," Kenneth said, trying not to show how affected he was by the possibility of Rebecca crying when he told her the truth. That would be horrid. And exactly what he deserved.

"But I am honest," Malcolm said with a single shrug of his shoulder. "Virtue for virtue, I might be ahead of you."

Chapter Thirteen

"Father," Rebecca said, coming to the table with a plate of cinnamon buns she'd warmed in the oven. Her throat was tight, but she pushed through it as she set down the plate and sat across from him. "We need to have a conversation."

Father paused in reaching for a bun, looking up at her. "What about?"

She hated that she was *this* nervous to talk to him. "I have been very grateful for your accommodation here these last years, especially regarding giving Rose a stable place after David's passing. I am concerned, however. You seem very unhappy." Her heart was thundering as hard as the rain beating against the windows. A summer storm had set in, keeping them indoors and canceling the day's errands—creating the perfect opportunity for her to broach this conversation.

"What is there to be happy about?"

Rebecca avoided the temptation to remind him of the good things about his life and stayed focused.

"You threw an ale mug at me, Father. It was—"

"I was angry," he said evenly. He picked a bun from the pan and put it on his plate. "I had expected you to be here, and you were not. You knew how important the Harkness sitting was, and you disregarded it. Any man would have been angry."

He said it without any emotion while using his fork to cut a bite of the bun.

"You meant to hurt me."

He looked at her with a neutral expression. "Do you want me to apologize?" The patronizing tone of his voice brought heat into her chest and neck. She could not meet his eye. She showed strength in other situations on a regular basis, but with her father she was always a child.

"I *do* want you to apologize," she said. "And I want your word that it shall not happen again."

"Will you be late again? Will you interfere with my work by not doing your part?"

"Have I ever been late before, Father? Is lateness deserving of violence?"

"Violence." He scoffed and cut another bite of his bun. "I took you and Rose in when you had nowhere else to go, Rebecca. If you've a better situation, take it, but while you are under my roof, you will live up to your responsibilities."

Her insecurity faded as her anger and frustration built. She managed to look him in the eye. "Or you will throw things at me? Hurt me? I have managed your home and your studio for years, and you would treat me this way? Do I mean so little to you?"

He narrowed his eyes, and she forced herself not to look away. She had lived most of her life trying to avoid making him angry, but his increased drinking in recent months had made that harder to do. It was difficult to play a different part on the stage of their relationship, but something had shifted, and if the repair did not come from him, the change would have to come from her. She felt butterflies at the realization that she held some power over the situation.

"You ungrateful, stupid woman!"

Rebecca startled at the intensity of his bellow.

He suddenly stood, grabbed the edge of the table, and flipped it toward her, causing the buns, cups of hot tea, and dishes to slide across the top into her lap.

She screamed and jumped out of the way, but her dress caught on the chair, and she fell into a heap on the ground. She lost track of Father's words as he continued to yell and berate her. She stayed on the floor, arms over her head, as she struggled to take a full breath.

Breathe in, breathe out, she told herself, trying to keep her focus.

Something struck her shoulder.

Breathe in, breath out.

Something solid hit her back, and a cloud of ash rained down on her—the ash bucket from when she'd cleaned out the hearth that morning. She coughed as the ash filtered through her hair, into her mouth, and down the back of her dress. She stared at the stone floor in front of her, now dusted with the fine powder of yesterday's meals and cleaning, and she wondered if Father was disappointed there had been no hot coals in the bin.

She pushed herself to her feet, flakes of ash falling off her, though she was still coated in it, and looked at her father, who was standing on the other side of the overturned table looking angry and . . . satisfied.

"You are a monster," she said in a harsh whisper, feeling her tears make tracks through the fine ash on her cheeks. "I have done all I can to make your life easier, to make up for your unhappiness, and it has earned me this?"

"You will do as I say!" he said through clenched teeth.

"I will not." Her voice was surprisingly calm.

He stepped toward her, and she fled, moving faster than he could as she ran up the stairs to her room, closing and locking the door behind her. He followed her and banged on the door while repeating the diatribe he'd already unleashed upon her.

She took off the ash-covered dress, rolling it up to contain the worst of the mess before tucking it into the corner of her carpetbag from her closet.

She blocked Father's words as she wet a cloth and wiped the ash from her face and neck and hands, uncovering herself in the reflection of the glass as her tears continued to fall. She focused her complete concentration on every movement required to clean herself up so she did not revert to the feelings she'd had while she'd cowered on the kitchen floor.

She was finished here. Her time in her father's home was over.

Father stopped yelling and pounding, and she listened to him go down the stairs, then out the front door, slamming it behind him.

She put what was worth taking into the carpetbag. Shoes, stockings, dresses, a few books, the shawl David had given her. When she'd filled the bag, she opened the door slowly and cautiously, listening for any indication that Father might still be in the house.

Once convinced the house was empty, she left the room she had shared with Rose for eight years, went down the stairs, and paused a moment to look at the studio. She would miss working on the silhouettes. It had been a luxury to be a part of something so beautiful.

That was the only thing she would miss.

Chapter Fourteen

I am at the parsonage for now," Rebecca explained as she and Rose walked side by side down the road. It was the same road they had walked a couple of weeks earlier after Rebecca had kissed Mr. Henry. It was Saturday afternoon; on Tuesday she would see him again at Grover Park. Would she tell him what had happened with Father?

"Mrs. Rushford has helped me make some inquiries for work," she continued.

"Oh, Mother," Rose said, leaning her head against Rebecca's shoulder. "I am heartsick for this."

"Do not be heartsick," Rebecca said, turning her head to kiss her daughter's hair, emotion filling her chest. "I have known for some time that I needed to make a change. I will find something."

Rose lifted her head, and they continued to walk. "You never wanted to return to service," she said, her tone sad.

"I never wanted to return to service when you were at home with me," Rebecca corrected. "And I am beyond grateful that I had the time to be the mother I wanted to be. I have no regrets on that end, and it is alright if my world changes now. You are settled, and I am so proud of all you have accomplished. I shall find my way. I have a good reputation here in Wakefield, and Mr. and Mrs. Rushford are as excellent a reference as anyone. I will find a good place, and all will be well."

"It will be such long hours," Rose said.

Rebecca kept to herself that she'd already been putting in long hours at Father's house—hours Rose did not know about.

Rose knew Rebecca would cut out Father's sketches and transfer them to the wood or black paper as ordered by the clients. She did not know that Rebecca also did the detailed cutting, the setting, the framing in some cases, and the finish—tasks she did after Rose had gone to sleep to preserve Father's ownership of the work and avoid anyone asking why Father signed his name.

She took both of Rose's hands in hers. "I am looking forward to the change, Rose, and truly believe I am on the correct path." She'd reached that understanding after she'd washed the ash from her hair, cleaned her dress, and sat before the parsonage's hearth, staring at the flames and feeling a calm settle upon her. "I want you to believe that as well."

Rose looked at her, worried. They had the same green eyes, same shape of the nose, and a similar smile. There was David in Rose too, though—the slight divot in her chin and her broad forehead.

"What if you came to work at Grangeford?" Rose suggested. "We could be there together."

Rebecca shook her head. Not because she hadn't had the same thought, but because she had already followed the thought all the way through to the end. It was a new idea for Rose, but not for Rebecca.

"You would not want your mother working belowstairs," she said, shaking her head. "You are in a position of respect at Grangeford, and I won't interfere with that."

Rose pulled her eyebrows together. "You think I would be embarrassed?"

"I think you *should* be embarrassed," Rebecca said. She began walking, forcing Rose to fall into step beside her.

"Why? Because you are finding your way? That is a source of pride to me, not shame."

"There are castes in every household, Rose, and I would be one of the lowest if I came on as a maid. It will be bad enough that I will be belowstairs in some other household. I should never do so where you are exposed to the judgment of it."

"You have helped with dinners at Grangeford several times since I took my employment with the baroness," Rose said, her tone determined. "And Mrs. Lenning is expecting you to help with the Mabon Ball as you have in the past."

"Helping for a night here and there is very different than being part of the household," Rebecca said. "I shall find another place, though I will hope I can be on hand for the Mabon Ball. It is a grand night, even for the staff."

Rose went silent, pouting as they continued to walk. "What of Mr. Timoltson?" she finally said. "Is he still paying you calls?"

Rebecca shook her head rather than explain that she'd told Mr. Timoltson not to call any longer. Thinking of him made her think of Malcolm, and she hoped Rose didn't notice the flush in her cheeks.

She would not pin her hopes—she was far wiser than that—but neither would she give up the idea that maybe, just maybe, he was meant to be part of her future somehow, and their paths crossing as they had that day on the road was not merely a coincidence. She had been counting the days until they would meet at Grover Park. It was lovely to have something to look forward to amid the uncertainty she was feeling about her future.

She glanced ahead of them on the street. "There is the ribbon shop. Did you still want to get the new trimmings for that bonnet?"

"You are changing the subject, Mother," Rose said.

"Indeed," she said, pulling on Rose's arm as she picked up the pace of their steps. "Because we have quite exhausted the topic. Let us lose ourselves in bits and bobs for a few minutes, alright, my dear? There is more to life than worry. Let's spend some time on that."

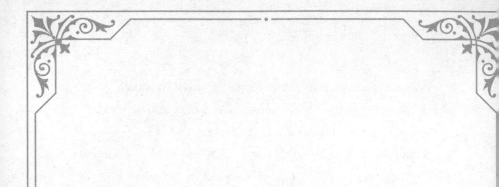

Chapter Fifteen

"And what did you think of Miss Huckstrom from the other night?" Uncle Lester asked after taking a bite of his mutton. It was just him and Kenneth for dinner tonight; Lady Beth always took the girls to the Langleys' home for Sunday dinner—a cousin on the late countess's side. Mr. Langley was far too modern for Uncle Lester's tastes, and Kenneth was glad to have a quiet evening once a week. Though he'd be even happier about that if Uncle Lester had chosen a different topic of discussion.

"She is very young," Kenneth said, also cutting his meat. The mutton was excellent tonight.

"You liked her, then?" Uncle asked.

"I liked her fine, for all of the fifty words we exchanged. But she is *very* young."

"That is a good thing," Uncle said, looking across the table at Kenneth with a confused look. "A young wife will be energetic and shall reflect well on you."

"She is nearly the age of my eldest son," Kenneth said, shaking his head. "It feels . . . perverse."

"Perverse!" Uncle repeated, sitting up straighter.

Kenneth put up a hand in apology. He knew better than to use such vulgar expressions and searched for another way to explain. "I would prefer a wife with similar life experience, that is all I mean."

"Why?" Uncle Lester looked truly dumbfounded.

"Because I want a wife I can talk with and relate to."

Uncle Lester's eyebrows pulled together as though trying to puzzle out the meaning behind Kenneth's explanation. "That makes absolutely no sense at all. The Huckstrom family is well established here and would be an excellent connection for you."

Kenneth sighed but also felt braver than usual. "I do not want to choose a wife simply because of her family connections."

"She is a lovely girl," Uncle Lester pointed out. "And I believe she likes horses. You like horses."

Hardly enough to base a marriage upon, Kenneth thought as he took another bite.

Uncle Lester continued, "You are a very odd man, Kenneth."

"Thank you."

"That was not a compliment!" He hit his hand against the table and then repeated what he had said a dozen times since Kenneth's arrival.

That Kenneth needed a wife from the local gentry.

That it was essential he get on with things.

That he had been given a great deal and very little was

required, so he ought to make short work of the task at hand and do his duty.

Kenneth continued to eat, glad he didn't feel the sense of discomfort he'd felt during previous lectures. He was getting used to Uncle Lester's intensity and opinions to the point where he could accept Uncle Lester's concern as an endearing trait. Irritating, yes, but also endearing.

"Well?" Uncle Lester said when he had apparently run out of words.

Kenneth finished chewing, then swallowed. "Miss Huckstrom is not the woman for me," he said simply.

Uncle Lester harrumphed. "What of Mrs. Trostle?"

"We had an interesting conversation about sheep," Kenneth said.

"She has one of the finest flocks in the county," Uncle Lester said admiringly. "Mr. Trostle, her late husband, began the flock, of course, but she has done an excellent job maintaining the livestock."

"Yes, it sounded like she is very devoted."

"So, you like her then?"

"Not enough to make her my wife," Kenneth said.

Uncle Lester growled in his throat. "Is there anyone you've met who you've even considered having as a wife?"

Rebecca, Kenneth said in his mind. He enjoyed talking with her, being with her. Kissing her. The shot of energy that memory brought to his chest caused him to shift in his chair. In two more days, he would see her again. Even though he knew he needed to tell her who he was. Even though it meant that whatever it was between them would be over.

"Well?" Uncle Lester pressed.

"No, Uncle," Kenneth said, sitting back in his chair, no longer hungry. "None of the women you have introduced me to have struck a chord."

"We shall run out of supply eventually," Uncle said, shaking his fork from his place across the table. "At which point, you shall have to decide from the ones you have already rejected!" He leaned back in his chair and his attitude softened, just a little. "I suggest you stop looking for a conversationalist and focus instead on who would make a good countess. Every marriage has its difficulties, regardless of who you choose. But choose you must. The sooner the better."

Chapter Sixteen

I am here," Rebecca announced as she entered the hot and bustling kitchen of Grangeford Monday evening. The cook turned from the stove, red-cheeked and foul tempered, her mobcap askew.

"It is about time!" the cook grumbled, turning back to her pots. "Plates go out in ten minutes."

Rebecca chose not to defend herself. She had received the note from Mrs. Lenning barely an hour ago and had sent a response that she would come as quickly as she could. She'd had an interview with the Campbell family on Remington Street that afternoon, and it seemed to have gone well, but they had not officially offered her the position yet. The wages she would receive for tonight's work would be welcome.

"Oh good, Mrs. Parker. You are just in time."

Rebecca turned and smiled at Mrs. Lenning. She'd been head maid when Rebecca had worked here all those years ago, though the staff called her by her first name back then. It had not surprised Rebecca when she'd heard of Mrs. Lenning's promotion to housekeeper two years ago. She'd been working at Grangeford nearly thirty years by then.

"The uniforms are in the third cupboard," Mrs. Lenning said. "Find one that fits and be ready in ten minutes. You can change in my office."

"I'm sorry?" Rebecca asked, confused. "I am here to help in the kitchen."

"We are down a *footman*, not a kitchen maid. If you help Nathan serve, Richard can manage the wine." She walked ahead to the third cupboard and pulled a charcoal-gray dress and starched white apron from the hooks inside. She turned and held out the items to Rebecca.

"I have not served for . . . well, years, Mrs. Lenning."

"But you are mature, capable, and you know the house." She shook the uniform she was still holding.

Rebecca took the clothes. It was one thing to be hidden away in the kitchen helping to prepare plates and stir sauces, quite another for her to serve as front of house.

Mrs. Lenning continued. "I had to fire the girl from the village, which means we are short *two* servants. The roast is too small, and the gravy curdled." She looked at Rebecca over her shoulder. "The evening is not going well, and we are all working beyond our usual places tonight. I need you to serve."

Rebecca leaned in and asked softly, "Is Rose to be included with the party?" She didn't want to embarrass her daughter.

"Not tonight," Mrs. Lenning said with equal softness and

appreciated understanding. "She was given the evening off and is paying a visit to Miss Hurley."

Rebecca let out a grateful breath and headed toward Mrs. Lenning's office to change into her uniform.

Twenty minutes later, Rebecca followed behind Nathan and matched his movements through the dining room. She repeated the serving instructions over and over to keep from missing anything: *serve from the left, no eye contact, say nothing, step back quickly.*

She and Nathan worked well together through the soup course and the salad. There were eighteen guests at the dinner, a good-sized party for so early in the week, but that was the extent of Rebecca's curiosity. She focused on her work amid the sound of overlapping conversations, clinking dishes, and punches of laughter as the wine flowed more and more freely.

Richard was doing a fine job keeping everyone's glass topped off. More than anything else, the wine would help the guests from noticing that the meat portion would be small and that there was a maid in the dining room instead of the handsome young men who were the usual attendants.

After the salad plates were cleared, Nathan held the tray of fish plates while Rebecca leaned in from the left to set the plates in front of each guest. The guests naturally leaned back to accommodate the serving, keeping everything running smoothly.

Only three more courses to go, Rebecca thought. They were halfway through!

As Rebecca leaned into the left of a woman with an

enormous ostrich feather in her hair, the woman flung her hand up unexpectedly, knocking the plate from Rebecca's hand.

The plate flew up amid a collective gasp, flipped the fish onto the tablecloth, and was on its way to crash into the woman's wineglass when Rebecca leaned forward and caught the plate before it landed. Without pausing, Rebecca used her other hand to scoop the fish from the table onto the plate she'd caught, then she turned and left the room.

The entire action took all of five seconds, but her cheeks flamed hot for having drawn the attention of the guests. The tablecloth was soiled, but there was no way to repair it in the middle of the meal. She would bring a washcloth and do as best she could.

Rebecca hurried into the kitchen, deposited the plate, and moved to the basin to wash the fish grease from her hands.

"I need another fish," she said to the cook as she dried her hands on a towel beside the sink.

"What do you mean you need another fish?" Cook said with a scowl, brandishing a knife like it was a sword she was prepared to use to cut out Rebecca's heart.

Unlike the kitchen maid and younger staff, Rebecca was not cowed by the woman's intensity. Cook was nothing compared to Father's rages, and it was easy to ignore this woman's sourness without taking any of it personally.

"There was an accident with one of the fish plates. We need a new one."

Cook grumbled and turned back to the stove.

Nathan came into the room with the now-empty tray.

"I am so sorry," Rebecca said, hurrying toward him so she could take the tray. It seemed to be the least she could do. "I did not know what to do, and I left you there to serve the remaining plates on your own."

"That was amazing!" he said, grinning.

"What was amazing?" Mrs. Lenning asked, bustling into the kitchen. Even she had donned a kitchen apron for the evening.

"Mrs. Collins knocked the plate from Rebecca's hand, and she caught it!"

Mrs. Lenning put a hand to her chest, and her brown eyes went wide. "Mrs. Collins caught the plate?"

"No," Nathan said, pointing at Rebecca. "Rebecca did. Caught the plate and cleared the fish before anyone knew what had happened. She moved so fast!"

Mrs. Lenning turned toward her. Rebecca did not meet her eyes, even more embarrassed, though she appreciated Nathan's validation.

"Is the new plate ready?" Rebecca asked after an awkward moment of appraisal from the housekeeper.

The cook handed her a new plate of fish, which Rebecca took with a nod. She grabbed a cloth from the sink and left the room before any more discussion could be had. She'd done what anyone would have done if they had been close enough.

When Rebecca entered the dining room with the fresh plate, every head turned to look at her and conversation stilled. Drawing attention from the servants was uncomfortable enough, having the attention of these distinguished persons was horrid.

"That was exceptional," the baroness said as Rebecca hurried toward the one place at the table that still lacked fish; Nathan had served Mrs. Collins already. The man with the empty place leaned to the side to accommodate her setting the plate before him. She wished that the guests would go back to ignoring her.

The room stayed silent. Were they expecting her to respond to the baroness? What on earth would she say?

"That truly *was* remarkable," Mrs. Collins said. "If that plate had hit my glass, I'd have been doused with red wine, which, I assure you, is far less enjoyable when it is upon one's clothes."

Rebecca looked across the table at the woman, recognizing Mrs. Collins by the ostrich feather. She smiled at Rebecca, a kind smile that requested a response.

"Thank you, ma'am," Rebecca said as she straightened. She stepped back, rethinking her plan of going around to make sure the tablecloth was clean, when she met the eyes of the man sitting next to Mrs. Collins.

Rebecca's mouth fell open as his name rose in her throat, but by the grace of God, the word did not reach her tongue. *Malcolm?*

At the baroness's table?

It was him.

But it was *not* him.

This man had Malcolm's face, his eyes—it *was* him—but he wore evening clothes. And a gentleman's valet would never sit at the table in company such as this. There was color in his face, which alerted her to the fact that there was likely color in hers as well.

"I suppose Mr. Winterton owes you as much thanks as I do.

We likely would have shared that glass of wine," Mrs. Collins said with a laugh.

Mr. Winterton.

Malcolm's employer.

Her head and chest were suddenly a flurry of thoughts and sensations as realization hit like a series of fists. In that moment, she could not remember why she was in the room, and she wanted nothing more than to get away.

He had lied to her.

And he was watching her as she realized it.

Rebecca turned and left the room, almost running to get out of there as quickly as possible. In the hallway, she stopped and put a hand to her chest. Her breath was coming too fast.

"Mr. Winterton?" she whispered so as to hear something spoken out loud.

Not Malcolm.

Not a valet.

It was difficult to take a full breath, and she could feel the burn of tears behind her eyes, which made her angry—a blessed relief from the hurt. She grabbed hold of the emotion with both hands and twisted it around her fingers and wrists like yarn she did not want to slip away. How dare she shed tears for this man who had made a fool of her!

The sound of footsteps further down the hall reminded her that she was on staff tonight, which meant there was no time for her to process this now. She rolled her shoulders back and took a deep breath while thinking about the night ahead. It would be a few more hours before she would leave for home. She could keep herself together until then, but not if she had to see him again. Fortunately, she was skilled in hiding her emotions and getting through difficult moments.

She would not go into the dining room again, however. Seeing him there was more than she could bear. She reached behind her back and untied the apron, taking it from around her neck as she headed in the direction of the kitchen. The dropped fish allowed her to excuse herself from serving in the dining room because she'd broken the rule about servants remaining unseen and unnoticed. That fallen fish had become her saving grace.

For a little while, at least.

Chapter Seventeen

Kenneth could not breathe as he met Rebecca's eyes from across the table. Could not think clearly. *She* was the maid who had saved Mrs. Collins's dress? The maid who had been in and out all evening?

He hadn't paid attention because men of his station did not look at the servants. But it was *her*. And him. Together in company that set their differences into sharp contrast. It had not been a maid he had taken no account of. It had been Rebecca. The one woman he could not stop thinking about. The last woman he expected to see tonight.

For a few seconds, the whole world froze, and then color came into Rebecca's face. A moment later, she turned and left the room as quickly as she'd caught that plate a few minutes before. His breathing became shallow, and his palms began to sweat.

The door closed behind her, and conversation around the

table returned, but Kenneth did not feel in complete control of his faculties.

"Are you alright, Mr. Winterton?" the baroness asked.

Kenneth looked toward her and realized a few other guests were watching him as well. He forced a smile and hoped it looked believable.

"Yes, sorry, my apologies."

The baroness held his eyes a second longer, then nodded and turned to the man seated on her left.

"Do you agree, Mr. Winterton?" Miss Longstone asked. She was seated on his other side.

Kenneth turned toward her. "I'm sorry, I lost my place—what do I think about what?"

"Our countryside. It is it very different from where you come from, is it not?"

"Oh, um, yes," he said, turning to the plate before him and trying to reconnect to this moment.

Fish.

Almost gone.

Had it been good?

"It is very . . . green, here," he said, then groaned internally. All of England was green this time of year.

What was Rebecca thinking right now?

What must she be feeling?

He wanted to go after her and explain. But what would he say? "Yes, I lied to you about who I was, and I kept up the lie when we met again."

They were supposed to meet tomorrow; he'd been planning

to reveal the truth then. In his growing imagination of the scene, he saw himself telling her, her being shocked—perhaps angry—but ultimately understanding. That was where the fantasy faded, though, because he could not see the next step.

He could not court her.

Unless he could.

But he couldn't.

She knew his lies now, and he felt as though his chest was full of stones while his mind was full of questions. What was she doing here? Was she a servant at Grangeford? If she had lied about her situation, did that justify his dishonesty?

Of course not.

It took a great deal of energy to maintain any semblance of interest in the conversation with Miss Longstone. It was a relief when she turned to the person on her other side.

Every time a servant entered the room, Kenneth looked up in both hope and fear. It was never her. She did not come back when the entrée was served, or the pudding. The women went on to the drawing room while the men enjoyed port and cigars and slightly bawdier talk. When the men joined the ladies later, Kenneth looked for Rebecca in the hallways. He saw the housekeeper and two footmen, but not a maid. No Rebecca.

He remained disconnected from the gathering and the conversations by the looping thoughts of how he could make this right.

Send a letter—but where?

Beg her forgiveness—how?

Make it up to her—utterly impossible.

It was a relief when his uncle finally ordered the carriage and they could give their goodbyes. That Jacqueline talked the entire ride back to the house was an additional blessing. He said good night to the family at the base of the stairs and then hurried to his room in the tower, charging in with enough energy that Malcolm startled to his feet from where he was sitting in front of the fireplace reading a book.

"Goodness, what's happened?"

Kenneth groaned as he pulled at his cravat. All the nerves in his body remained on high alert.

"What is wrong with you?" Malcolm said, eyebrows furrowed.

"Rebecca!" he said, pulling harder at the fabric around his neck. He felt as though he were choking. "She was there! Serving dinner." He pictured her in his head—maid's uniform, white mobcap, her blonde hair escaping in a few curls. The look on her face when she'd realized the truth.

He'd undone the knot in his cravat incorrectly, and it was stuck. He tugged hard, which merely tightened the knot.

"What was she doing there?" Kenneth asked as though Malcolm would know.

Malcolm pulled Kenneth's hands away from the knotted cravat. He began easing it out of the tangle. "Are we talking about *my* Rebecca?" he asked.

Fire ignited in Kenneth's belly, but he couldn't argue with him. He knew Malcolm was only trying to bait him. Kenneth closed his eyes, feeling sick and frustrated while Malcolm continued to untangle the cravat.

"She saw me there," Kenneth said, Rebecca's green eyes burned into his memory. "She knows I lied to her."

"Which you knew would happen."

"I did," he admitted, resisting the impulse to cover his face with his hands as though he could hide from what a scoundrel he was. "But I did not expect to see her realization. Her face . . ." He saw it again, the way her expression showed surprise, then confusion, then absolute humiliation in a single second.

"What happened?" Malcolm asked, finally undoing the knot and working to unwrap it from Kenneth's collar.

Kenneth stepped away, still not used to being dressed and undressed by another man. He paced as he unwound the cravat himself and then began unbuttoning his waistcoat. He dropped it to the bed, and Malcolm picked it up, putting it over his arm with the cravat. Kenneth continued to pace as he took off the clothing that felt so suffocating while recounting the experience. Malcolm continued to pick up discarded clothing but said nothing until, finally, Kenneth wore only his shirt, which hung to his knees.

"That is unfortunate, Winterton. I am sorry that happened."

Kenneth crossed his arms and let out a deep breath as he turned to look out the window. He could see the lights of the village and wondered which pinpoint of light was her father's home. Or was she in the servants' quarters of Grangeford? What was she doing right now? How was she feeling?

"How can I explain myself to her?" Kenneth asked as Malcolm joined him at the window. "How can I fix this?"

"Not everything can be fixed," Malcolm said, his tone sympathetic even if the words were hard to hear.

Chapter Eighteen

A re you sure you don't want me to walk with you?" Rose
asked from the doorway of the kitchen, looking skepti-
cally at the night sky beyond the yard.

"I am sure," Rebecca said, giving Rose a final embrace. "I
know the way and am quite safe. It is a warm night and a nearly
full moon."

Rose had returned to Grangeford near the end of dinner and
entered the kitchens in order to take a plate of pudding to her
room. She'd been surprised to find her mother there. By then,
Rebecca had already recognized Malcolm—not-Malcolm—and
refused to return to the dining room, claiming she was too embarrassed over the spilled fish and would be a distraction for the
guests.

Mrs. Lenning had argued the point, but Rebecca had held
her ground, tightening up every muscle in her body to prevent
herself from reacting to the emotional thunderstorm brewing in

her belly. She'd learned the skill from years of dealing with her father, though she was not grateful for the practice.

"Shall we meet for a walk on Friday?" Rose asked Rebecca.

"I am to visit with the Campbells that day for a second interview," she said, though Friday felt forever away. "Saturday?"

"Saturday, then," Rose said with a nod and a smile. She was so confident, so elegant.

It made Rebecca both happy to see the growth and a little sad to see the young Rose slipping away. It was inevitable, living in a noblewoman's household and socializing with a higher level of people. People like . . . Mr. Winterton.

Rose gave Rebecca another quick hug, then they wished one another good night.

Rebecca followed the path from the kitchen yard that would lead her to the parsonage half a mile away. It cut through the woods, but the night was mild. She focused on her breathing, which was coming faster now that she was alone.

When the path passed near the huge walnut tree, Rebecca stopped for a moment. The tree was a landmark for the Konold estate, standing almost dead center of the property. It had likely been there for ages, its bark rough and its branches wide.

She sat at the base of the tree, resting her back against the trunk, feeling the physical exhaustion catching up to her. She was grateful for a moment to rest. More than that, she was grateful to be alone, finally, and to reflect in private on what had happened.

Rebecca closed her eyes and let herself remember that moment of holding his eyes across the table. Seeing the realization in his face just as he was seeing the realization in hers. What an idiot she was for having thought Malcolm was real. Her chin quivered, and she raised her hands to cover her face as both humiliation and sadness filled all the spaces inside her. She had used that kiss, and the connection she'd felt from it, as a reason not to encourage Mr. Timoltson's interest, as proof that there was something more for her. She'd built it up into something magical and looked at Malcolm as a possibility.

It was all lies.

The walk in Grover Park where she'd felt so trusted with his story.

Lies.

The feeling of connection she'd had learning about his insecurity with his personal journey to a new position in a new part of the country.

Lies.

She'd been looking forward to meeting him at the park again tomorrow, expecting to feel even closer to him.

And then what? What was his goal?

The emotions she'd kept tamped down rose, making her head ache and her throat burn. She gave into the tears and let herself cry for a minute, maybe two, but then found she lacked the energy to lose herself in the sorrow. The tears dried up. The feeling of depletion settled like snow upon her head and shoulders.

What did it matter? What good would it do to feel hurt over such a man?

She hadn't pinned her hopes on *Malcolm*, even though she'd

let herself fantasize about the possibility—which now, she realized, had never been real.

He'd known that from the first moment he'd seen her on the side of the road. From the moment he'd kissed her.

Her cheeks flamed to have been so foolish. She'd been so open with him and felt so understood. The loss of that was perhaps the most painful part. She'd trusted him and felt enlivened by him, but it was nothing at all. Never had been.

She sat against the tree, head in her hands, until she was too exhausted to feel anything at all. She pushed herself to standing, then picked up a few walnuts from last season. She moved toward the path and turned, lined up a specific striation of the bark, and threw the walnuts, one right after the other, at the spot, hitting it square on every time, pretending she was hurting him the way she had been hurt.

Rebecca had always had excellent aim and a steady hand, and when the walnuts were gone, she thought on that for a moment. Excellent aim was not so different from setting a goal and ensuring she completed it. A steady hand could be any manner of steadiness, and she'd proved well enough in her life that she possessed that ability too. Every time the ground beneath her feet began to crumble, she'd found her way through.

What was she to learn from this?

"Life is not fair," she said out loud as she rejoined the path that would take her to the parsonage where she was being housed like a refugee. Yet, even in the trench of self-pity, she felt gratitude to have a place. Life was not necessarily *unfair*. No one had a simple existence, though some had more ease than others.

She had first realized that when she'd worked in the baroness's household and seen the difficulties each member of the family faced as they too tried to learn their place. The baroness's son, now the baron, though he had not lived at Grangeford for years, had been headstrong and difficult from childhood. The baroness's marriage, though a strong one, had its share of arguments and disputes that would linger for days sometimes.

She had watched the baroness rise to her position every day, even when she felt unwell, even when she'd been awake half the night with worry or planning the next event. More ease, yes, but more responsibility too. Rebecca did not desire that life, though there were aspects she admired. So, saying that life was not fair did not give her peace or strengthen her resolve to feel neutral about Mr. Winterton's trick. No one's life was necessarily fair.

"Trust no one," she said as she tightened the shawl around her shoulders, grateful for the moonlight on the path before her. That new summation did not sit right with her either. Only one man had lied to her, tricked her, made her feel like a fool. That did not mean other people would do the same.

"Learn," she finally said, and the word settled in her chest like it belonged there. No one was going to save her from the hardships of life, but she did not need them to. She was capable, she was strong, she was determined, and she was good. Those qualities had served her well and would continue to do so.

There was no Prince Charming, no carriage to whisk her away, no Malcolm. Her choices were her own. With David gone and Rose raised into as fine a young woman as Rebecca could ever hope for, Rebecca's journey belonged only to herself now.

She would take the position with the Campbells and apply herself to diligent work she could take pride in. There was nothing she could do to change the circumstances of her life, but she could do her best within it. She could show God her willingness to work hard and serve well. Somehow, everything would turn out.

She *had* to believe in that. Now more than ever.

Chapter Nineteen

Kenneth kept their appointment to meet at the park, even though he was sure Rebecca would not show. If he were in her position, he did not think he would either, but he felt desperate to talk to her and did not know how else to do it.

He arrived half an hour before the appointed time, dressed as Malcolm, and waited another half an hour past the appointment time before he left. While he waited, he reviewed every exchange they'd had, seeing her expression over and over again when she'd realized who he was.

The need to explain himself nipped at his heels as he headed back to the public stable and fetched Thunderbolt. He paid the groom and walked Thunderbolt a safe distance down the road, so the horse would not frighten anyone. When he was alone, Kenneth launched himself onto the animal's back and braced for the jolt forward, which did not disappoint.

He did all he could to keep the animal in check while on

the roads, the memory of the first time he'd seen Rebecca's wide green eyes stark in his mind, but when he reached a path through an open field, he let Thunderbolt live up to his new name.

Pressed against the animal's neck, Kenneth wished the wind could pull his regrets from his mind, and yet it wasn't fair that he should simply be absolved of what he'd done. He *had* done wrong—behaved badly. Why should he simply feel better about that because he wanted to feel better?

As the wind burned his cheeks, he thought back to what Malcolm had said about some things being unfixable. Even if he had the chance to explain himself to Rebecca, even if she forgave him, he could not fix the reasons he'd lied in the first place. He had expectations to fulfill, a position to secure, and a life to build here in Wakefield. He needed a wife who would feel comfortable in her place and help him fulfill his responsibility.

He hated that Rebecca was not that woman, and that the woman who *was* right for the position of countess might not have the same connection he felt with Rebecca. Perhaps it was selfish and juvenile to want everything, but that was exactly what he wanted—a countess he could adore and connect with like a friend.

He pushed Thunderbolt even harder to make up for the regret he felt realizing he would have to choose one or the other.

Except the choice had already been made.

He had responsibilities to his uncle and to the fortune that had come his way, and those responsibilities would win.

He could not be with Rebecca.

Worse, he would likely never have the chance to apologize to her.

She was the ultimate victim of the whole messy situation. It was so unfair to her, and there was nothing he could do to fix it.

Chapter Twenty

Rebecca shifted awkwardly in her chair in the parlor of the parsonage and tried not to look too closely at Father's face as the parson explained the need for love and kindness in all relationships.

During the years Rebecca had attended school, she'd never been sent to the headmistress's office to be reprimanded, but she imagined it felt a lot like this. Except she was forty-two years old, and it was Father being reprimanded, albeit kindly. She, instead, was in the role of tattletale. Her palms were sweating, and it was hard to keep from bouncing her feet as a release of her anxiety. Honestly, she was surprised Father had agreed to come at all.

"I do not *need* Rebecca to take care of me," Father said when the parson asked for his side of things. "If she does not want to be in my home, so be it." He shrugged, and Rebecca swallowed.

When she had come to the parsonage, she had simply told

the Rushfords that she and her father were not getting on and that she needed a place to stay. She hadn't mentioned the violence she had experienced at her father's hand, and she certainly wasn't going to bring it up now.

She was quite sure Father had realized what she'd left out, and that kept him from being too amplified as well. It appeared her attempt to protect everyone would remain intact. Truth be told, she had not felt this meeting was a good idea, but Mr. Rushford had so wanted to help repair things between them, and after the generosity Mr. and Mrs. Rushford had given her, she did not see how she could say no.

"I do, however, need some help with my work."

Rebecca and the parson exchanged glances before the parson looked back at Father. "Please explain," Mr. Rushford asked, leaning forward slightly as he seemed to recognize the opportunity for repair.

Father explained that Lady Beth had come to the studio earlier in the week and set an appointment for all three of her daughters on Thursday next—a week from today.

"I cannot manage three sittings on my own," Father said.

"I am happy to help," Rebecca said, relieved at the idea that they might maintain some connection without animosity.

She loved working on the silhouettes, and perhaps this might be the bridge they could build between one another. When David had been alive, Rebecca had gone to the studio a few days a week to help Father with the transfer work. He had not been kind then either, but better than recent years. The thought that they might preserve their relationship even that much was encouraging.

"Assuming I am able to arrange it with the Campbells, if I have started working by then, what time should I be there?"

"Eleven," Father said as he stood, apparently finished with the interview. He turned to the door and retrieved his hat.

Mr. Rushford hurried around the desk to show him out. "Thank you for coming in, Mr. Seffton, and for the presence of mind to see all perspectives in this situation. Family is God's great gift to us."

Father looked at the parson coldly, then turned the icy look to Rebecca. He held her eyes a moment, then let himself out without another word.

"How do you feel the meeting went, Mrs. Parker?" the parson asked when they'd finished. He was not an old man, only ten years or so Rebecca's senior, and she could tell by his expression that he felt it had been a success.

"I am pleased," she said, which was true. That Father had come at all had been surprising. That he'd accepted she was not returning to his home and had asked for her help to continue his work—those were good things too. His cold look at the end left her unsettled, but not enough to override the good that had taken place. "Thank you very much, Mr. Rushford. I think we will be better for this and appreciate your efforts."

Chapter Twenty-One

Another evening. Another dinner party. Another eligible woman in attendance who did not inspire Kenneth's interest.

He'd drunk too much wine at dinner and then too much port with the men after the women had left, which made his head muddled by the time the men returned to the drawing room. He asked the footman standing by the door to fetch some strong tea and refused the scotch offered by the other footman.

He sat rather heavily in one of the chairs near the fireplace, wishing he could forgo the rest of the evening and retreat to his tower room. He would open his sketchbook and draw dark, thick lines of a face with heavy-lidded eyes, a black night sky. He would open the window and hope the night air would sober him up, and then he would sleep the sleep of a dead man and find his only solace.

It had been four days since the baroness's dinner party, and he still saw the look on Rebecca's face every time he closed his eyes. Malcolm had tried to help him justify his actions and let go of his self-blame, but Kenneth was having a difficult time doing so.

"Are you alright?"

Kenneth turned his head to see Lady Beth had taken the chair beside him. She sat on the edge of the chair, back straight, a glass of sherry in her hand, which made him aware of his own slumped posture, elbow on the armrest and head on his hand. He pulled himself up to a more respectable form, embarrassed to be seen in such a state, while also not caring one whit.

"Yes, Lady Beth, I am fine."

She leaned toward him slightly. "Are you certain? If you are ill, you may excuse yourself. I will support your complaint with my father."

"Thank you, but I've just had too much to drink at dinner. Watson is fetching me some strong tea."

She nodded, then looked past him and smiled wider. "Mrs. Taylor," she said, then waved toward the open settee next to Kenneth's chair. "I must say that your gown is remarkable tonight. Is that hand beading?"

Mrs. Taylor was tonight's showcased countess-to-be, and Kenneth looked at her dress for the first time. It was a blue dress, which made him think of Rebecca and the blue dress she'd worn the day he'd nearly run her over on the road. That kiss. The feeling of her hands pressing against his and the urgency of their connection.

He shook his head physically to force the thoughts away.

The dresses weren't even the same shade of blue. Mrs. Taylor had sat next to him all through dinner and long stretches of silence had passed between them.

"It is a lovely dress . . . er, gown," Kenneth said.

Lady Beth gave him an encouraging smile, which boosted his confidence.

"Are the beads glass?" he asked.

The tea came, he drank it studiously, grateful that Lady Beth stayed close, leading the conversation as needed and helping him not give the impression of a complete idiot or a drunk. Or both. When the company left, Kenneth was able to walk the party to the door and send them off almost without feeling as though he were acting a part in a play.

He turned toward his tower room to find Lady Beth standing in the hall. "I am guessing Mrs. Taylor did not draw your interest."

"None of the women who have paraded through this drawing room or were seated by me at dinner this last month have drawn my interest."

"Perhaps you are too particular."

He nodded his head. "Perhaps."

"Father says you are looking for a love match."

Kenneth shrugged, his tongue still loose from the wine and frustration. "I suppose I am a romantic."

"Your first wife, then—you were happy with her?"

Kenneth thought about that, surprised by Lady Beth's interest. They had never spoken of such topics before, but he could think of no reason to be dishonest.

"We never had much of an opportunity to find our place," he explained, hating that his first wife—Lydia—felt like such a distant memory. "Christopher was born while I was in Spain. I came home for nearly a year after, and Lydia was expecting Jeremy by the time I left again." He looked at the tiled floor at his feet. It felt like a lifetime ago.

"She had been gone almost a month before I learned of Jeremy's birth and her passing. I was relieved of my position almost immediately, so I could return to the estate and my motherless sons. In many ways I feel as though I barely knew her. I want a different sort of match this time."

"One might wonder why you never remarried," Lady Beth mused, leaning against the wall in the hallway, as casual a pose as he'd ever seen her take.

"One might wonder the same of you."

"Oh, I doubt anyone truly wonders of that for me," Lady Beth said with a laugh, waving her hand through the air. "I have no reason to remarry. My needs are met."

He nearly asked if *all* her needs were met, but that would be improper and perhaps suggestive, which was the last direction he wanted to take. Lady Beth was tall and angular, with a heavy brow and a small chin. Beyond that, there was a hardness to her personality. She was driven and dependable and an excellent hostess, but there was nothing soft about her. Nothing warm and inviting. Kenneth had never felt the least bit of attraction to her.

"You do not miss having a partner?" he asked.

"Heaven's no," she said with another laugh. "Wives are

rarely partners. We are figureheads, arm dressings, and hostesses. It is our job to make the man, so to speak."

What a sad belief, Kenneth thought, but then wondered why he thought differently. It was not as though he had seen many marriages that reflected what he wanted—partnership, attraction, camaraderie. "Do you really think so?" Perhaps he was not only a romantic, but an impossible one. Perhaps what he wanted was pure fiction.

She paused as though gathering her thoughts. "Mr. Winterton," she said kindly. "Men need wives in order to be capable of the responsibility placed upon them. Men who suddenly find themselves in situations like yourself, with responsibility and trusts to uphold, are especially needful. I cannot say I understand why your expectation of marriage is so different from others, but I *can* tell you the right wife will make your life a much more comfortable endeavor."

"And the wrong wife?" Kenneth asked.

She held his eyes a moment. "Not a single woman you have been introduced to thus far would be the wrong wife. That is my point. Any one of them would afford you the respect and support you need to be successful in your place. Any one of them would be a credit to you."

"And the fact that I feel nothing toward them?"

"Is because you are not yet committed," Lady Beth said without hesitation. "It is after the commitment—which should be made based on ideals and breeding—that feelings grow. I married a man thirty years my senior, Mr. Winterton, and we grew in accord and respect each day of our marriage. My parents had met once before they married, and they spent nearly forty years together. I daresay they came to love each other very much. Had they judged that possibility the most important one upon their initial impressions, they may have chosen a course less desirable for both of them."

Kenneth remembered Lady Brenston from when he was a child and would visit Brenning Hall, back when he had no expectation that he would one day be master of the place. He rarely saw his uncle and aunt together, and when he did, they were formal. She had called him Lord Brenston, and he had called her Lady Brenston. Perhaps his expectation of what such a marriage should look like *was* incorrect, or perhaps there had been a closeness that a ten-year-old boy did not notice.

Lady Beth pushed herself up from the wall, reclaiming her straight-backed formality. "It is none of my business, of course. Only you seem . . . tense about the decision. I know my father can be demanding and harsh, but he does want what is best for you, and I agree that a wife will help your progress in the community tenfold. If there is anything I might do to help you in the decision, please let me know. I am familiar with all of these women and would consider it an honor to assist you in the vetting process."

"Vetting," he repeated, shaking his head as he remembered his father using the same word to describe which horses would be kept for breeding stock and which would be sold to second-rate horsemen.

"It *is* what you are doing, Mr. Winterton," Lady Beth said, cocking her head sympathetically to one side. "Comparing, choosing characteristics. I daresay the way to make the best choice would be to keep your feelings out of the decision entirely and focus wholly on how each woman would represent you and the interests of the earldom. Trust that the emotional connection will grow in time."

It was disheartening to be so misunderstood, but then he wondered if he was the one without understanding. Perhaps he truly did not know how things were done in the circles he now found himself in. "Thank you, Lady Beth. I appreciate your concern and shall consider your thoughts."

She smiled, which improved her features some. "For what it is worth, Mr. Winterton, I believe you will be an excellent earl one day. I was not so sure of that after Edward died." She looked away from him, sorrow in her eyes. "My brother was such a good man."

"And born for the role," Kenneth added, also thinking of his cousin. Edward had received top marks in everything he'd done—school, university, polo. He had been good with people, invested in politics, and a solid heir to the earldom. Kenneth often felt the comparison of Edward's excellence to his own mediocrity.

"But he put off marriage," Lady Beth added, drawing Kenneth's attention back to her. "The argument you are having within yourself is the same argument Edward had with my father for years. He did not want to settle. He did not want to make a wrong choice.

"In the end, he was nearly forty years old and left no heir. My father not only lost his only son, he also lost his legacy and assurance that the earldom would continue to be the vestiture he had spent his life procuring. That is not to say he is disappointed that you will inherit after him—he is impressed with your determination—but you are stuck in the same place Edward was and that creates a great deal of discomfort for my father."

Kenneth had never thought of it that way. Of course, Uncle Lester had been devastated about Edward's death, the mere thought of burying one of his own sons made Kenneth's lungs freeze in his chest.

He hadn't considered, however, how that loss had affected Uncle Lester regarding the heraldry. His title, which he had worked his life to build and protect, had shifted dramatically upon Edward's passing. The line for every other earl of Brenston moved from Uncle Lester to his younger brother, Kenneth's father, already ten years passed, and then to Kenneth himself. Kenneth's sons would receive the title from him, but their preparation would be Kenneth's responsibility. Whatever he did with his place would affect the line forever.

Kenneth said good night to Lady Beth and continued to his room in a thoughtful state of mind. He'd been so focused on his own situation and his shift in fortune that he had not realized the full burden his uncle carried nor the spectrum of loss he had experienced. To think that Kenneth's hesitations to find a wife were a further burden to his uncle saddened him. He vowed to do better.

He let himself through the door that led to the base of the tower stairs, letting it close behind him. Alone, surrounded by brick and mortar, he whispered, "Rebecca is lost to you. She was never a consideration, even if she was, perhaps, a distraction for a time."

He let the words bounce around the stairwell and reverberate back to him. They were painful to say, but they had to be said. Had to be accepted and acknowledged fully.

He climbed the stairs to his room and let himself in, grateful that Malcolm had given up on him already.

"It is done," he said out loud as he removed his coat.

He truly believed it.

Chapter Twenty-Two

T hank you so much for accompanying the girls to this appointment, Mr. Winterton," Lady Beth said as she helped herd her three daughters toward the front door of Brenning Hall. "I did not feel right sending them without supervision."

"It is my pleasure, Lady Beth," he said, following behind her. He and Lady Beth had established a more comfortable place since their talk in the hallway last week. Though she did not agree with his reasons for being so particular in his choice of wife, neither had she shamed him or tried to bully him into seeing things her way. He'd thought a great deal about their conversation and was happy to extend a favor when her girls needed a chaperone.

Lady Beth stopped at the threshold, hands clasped to her chest. The grateful smile on her angular face did not make her any more beautiful, but did at least soften the hard lines.

"I am happy to be of assistance," Kenneth said as he helped

the girls into the carriage. Then he tipped his hat to Lady Beth and stepped inside, pulling the door closed behind him.

There was an empty space on the bench next to Jacqueline, the oldest of the three girls. He slid into the seat, and she instantly shifted closer to him. He looked at her in surprise, and she offered him a sweet, if not syrupy, smile. She held his eyes as she looped her arm through his and leaned into him even more.

Kenneth would often extend his arm to one of the girls when they were walking to dinner or outdoors together. They usually giggled or blushed when he offered such a grown-up action, and he felt like a kindly uncle helping them learn and practice the manners of their class. He'd never thought of it as anything other than a show of respect.

Jacqueline's behavior was different than any of those other interactions, and he quickly faced forward and swallowed. Jacqueline was beautiful and well-mannered, which was to be expected of an earl's granddaughter. But at nineteen years old, she was very much a child in his eyes. Did she not see him as a dusty old man?

"It is so kind of you to come with us, Mr. Winterton," she said in a tone she had never used with him before.

He carefully extracted his arm from hers, using the excuse of fiddling with his cuff as reason. He scooted further to the side, and she promptly moved closer to him again, leaving him against one side of the carriage, with her pressed against his other side and six inches of empty seat beside her.

Good gracious!

"I am excited to have my form and figure captured in

silhouette for all time," Jacqueline said, her tone unusually high, which to his ear made her seem even younger than she was— which was very, *very* young. "Mama says she shall hang them in the parlor so that all our guests will see them."

"I want mine hung in my room," Nancy pouted. She was the youngest at fifteen. She stuck out her bottom lip and began to kick her heel against the bench. "And I want it in a gold frame."

"Mama is having carved walnut frames made," said Cynthia, the seventeen-year-old and most formal of the three. She was usually the voice of reason within their squabbles and seemed more mature than Jacqueline. "They will be very elegant."

"You do not even know how to spell elegant," said Nancy, who was the youngest and most likely to have a muddy hem and pastries in her dress pockets.

Cynthia sighed and looked out the windows.

"Do you want me to spell it for you?" Nancy said. "It is spelled C-Y-N-T-H-I-A S-M-E-L-L-S L-I-K-E A P-I-G."

Kenneth turned toward the window to hide his smile, then groaned inside as Jacqueline slipped her arm through his again. All mirth disappeared. This was trouble. Lady Beth was his first cousin; he *could* marry her, though it would be frowned upon. Marrying her daughter, however, would not raise a single eyebrow. A match between them would be seen as an advantage to everyone. Except to him. A nineteen-year-old wife? A woman younger than both his sons with no experience of life? Not in a thousand years did he want such a woman.

Perhaps he would start wearing his spectacles more often to

further the impression that he was an old man. If he stopped shaving his head smooth and let his gray hair grow back in tufts over his ears, would that deter her interest?

When they arrived at the address of the artist doing the silhouettes, Kenneth jumped from the carriage as quickly as possible. Though still largely unfamiliar with Wakefield, he recognized this was not an affluent part of town. Rather, it was a place of tradesmen and craftsmen—the sort of street where the family lived in rooms above the storefront. There was a cobbler beside a silversmith shop on one side; he could hear the clanging of the blacksmith's hammer at the end of the block.

Their destination was a gray building with peeling paint around the doorframe and a freshly swept stoop. There was a hand-painted sign in the window that said "Seffton Shades" and had a simplified example of the black profiles Kenneth had seen in country homes from time to time.

Lady Beth had described the silhouettes, or shades as they were commonly called, as a primitive portraiture that was becoming all the rage. Those he'd seen were striking, the stark contrast of the light and dark creating an unexpected balance in the portraits. The process had to do with light and tracing that required the girls to come to the artist rather than the artist traveling to Brenning Hall. That was all he knew.

Jacqueline was the last of the girls he helped exit the carriage. When she attempted to put her arm through his again, he strode forward as though he did not notice. At the door, he knocked three times and put a pleasant smile on his face in preparation of meeting the artist, or perhaps the artist's wife.

The knob turned, the door opened, and Kenneth froze when he found himself staring into the green eyes that had been haunting him for weeks.

Rebecca looked back at him with an equally shocked expression.

They stood facing one another for one, two, three full seconds. Then she looked at the ground and said nothing.

"I, uh, hello. I am, uh, here for . . ." What was he here for?

It was difficult to concentrate under the barrage of memories racing through his mind of all the different situations he'd seen Rebecca in before today. She'd been wearing a blue dress on the day he'd run her off the road, a green and yellow one when they'd met at Grover Park, and a maid's uniform when they'd found themselves face to face at the baroness's dinner party more than two weeks ago.

Today she was dressed in a light-gray dress that buttoned up the front with sleeves that reached her wrists. Her hair was pulled up as it had always been. He had only seen it uncovered at their first meeting when she'd removed the ruined bonnet. It occurred to him that he should have replaced that bonnet, and he wished very much that he'd done so. Perhaps with a note telling her who he really was and apologizing for the deception, which, at that point, would have been minimal.

Cynthia stepped forward and said helpfully, "We are the Brenston granddaughters, and this is our mother's cousin, Mr. Winterton, heir presumptive to the Brenston title. We have sittings today for our profiles to be done with Mr. Seffton."

"Yes, of course," Rebecca said, nodding and smiling at

Cynthia, clearly grateful that someone had taken charge. "Please come in."

She stepped to the side and held the door open.

Kenneth stepped back, ushering the girls to enter ahead of him. Rebecca did not look at him as he passed her in the doorway; he felt like the greatest toad ever put upon the earth. He *had* to find a way to apologize at least, and explain himself if possible. The idea that this encounter was his chance for absolution helped soften the shame he'd been wrestling with. Surely, he would feel better if he could talk to Rebecca.

When he stepped inside the house, the girls were already in the studio. To his right was a parlor and to his left was a door that likely led to the apartments above.

He followed the short hall to the studio, which was a large room in the back with heavy drapes pulled open on the windows, and unlit gaslights set on posts throughout the room. A large white piece of paper was tacked against the wall, nearly floor to ceiling, a short wooden box in front.

Rebecca stood off to the side, her hands clasped as the girls looked around the room with expressions ranging from curiosity—Nancy—to judgment—Jacqueline.

He shifted his weight in hopes it would balance the invigoration and discomfort he was feeling. It did not help.

"Mr. Seffton is my father, and I assist him with his work," Rebecca said to the girls, though Kenneth suspected she had waited to say it to make sure he heard it. "He shall be here shortly. He always goes for a walk before a sitting to clear his head and enliven his senses. While we wait for him to return, let me explain how the process will work."

Each girl in turn would stand upon the wooden box in front of the paper. The thick curtains would be pulled, and the lights would be lit to cast the girl's shadow upon the paper behind them. Mr. Seffton would trace the outline upon the paper. After the tracing was finished, a pattern would be made that was half the size. That pattern would be carefully cut and traced onto a thicker piece of woven paper coated in black. Each image would be cut to the exact dimension of each of the silhouettes and mounted against a silk background, at which point they would be delivered to the framer to be set into the custom frames Lady Beth had ordered.

"I am afraid it can be a bit tedious to do the sitting," Rebecca explained. "It takes nearly thirty minutes for each sketch, and the lantern can become uncomfortably warm, but we will do all we can to ensure that things move quickly without sacrificing the quality of the work. Do you have any questions?"

When she raised her eyebrows at the girls, awaiting their response, Kenneth noticed the faint pink scar along her jawline, the legacy of their first encounter on the road. The desire to pull her aside and explain himself was difficult to resist, but they could not have any privacy in such a small space with three sets of curious eyes upon him.

"May I go first?" Jacqueline asked, stepping forward, chin lifted. "I get faint from the heat, you see, and might need Mr. Winterton to take me for a walk to refresh myself while my sisters have their turn."

"Actually, I think Nancy should go first," Kenneth said quickly, stepping forward with a slight jolt of panic at the idea of having individual time with Jacqueline. "She is the youngest and, therefore, the one with the shortest attention span."

"I do not have a short attention span!" Nancy snapped, then paused and her expression softened. "But I never get to be first."

Rebecca turned toward him but did not meet his eye. "There is a small parlor at the other end of the hallway where those not sitting can wait. I shall open the window so that the room stays cool."

"Excellent," Kenneth said gratefully, wishing she would look at him.

Jacqueline pouted. Not prettily.

"Of course, Mr. . . . Winterton," Rebecca said, the pause sounding like drumbeats. It was the first time she'd used his real name, and a heavy reminder of why she struggled to say it out loud. "I have prepared a tea tray for those waiting and have a selection of periodicals that might occupy your attention."

"Excellent, thank you, Mrs. Parker," Cynthia said with a nod.

"Which periodicals?" Jacqueline asked, not looking at Rebecca as she spoke, but instead inspecting the room again. It was well-appointed for an art studio—plain walls, nothing to distract the artist from his work. "I only read *The Marriage Gazette* and *Ladies Monthly Museum*," Jacqueline continued. "And I have, of course, already read the most recent editions."

Kenneth cringed at the rudeness. Did Jacqueline even notice her lack of manners? The squeak of a hinge from the front of the studio caused all of them to turn their heads, ending further conversation.

"Ah, here is Mr. Seffton now," Rebecca said.

The front door opened, and an elderly man with a gray beard walked past the group, who all stepped back to let him pass. He moved to one side of the room and began sharpening pencils laid out on a table. Kenneth was surprised the man said nothing in greeting. A quick glance at Rebecca made him think she was surprised too. She had two bright spots of color on her cheeks.

Rebecca cleared her throat, sounding uncomfortable for the first time. "Mr. Winterton, perhaps you could escort the other ladies into the parlor while I get Miss Nancy settled. I shall bring in the tea tray once my father has begun his work."

For a moment their eyes met, then she looked away. That moment was enough to renew Kenneth's desperation to explain himself. He wanted her to understand him. He wanted her forgiveness. He dared to hope such things were possible.

"Of course." Kenneth led Cynthia and Jacqueline through the narrow hallway to the parlor near the front of the house. This room was fancier than the studio with pale blue walls, bright curtains, and matching cushions on each of the chairs. As promised, there was a stack of magazines set upon the center table.

Kenneth moved toward the window, pulling it open to cool the room as Rebecca had suggested. Along with the breeze, the sounds of the street flowed into the room.

"I want the one with the blue cover," Jacqueline said.

He turned away from the window in time to see Cynthia

take the blue-covered periodical from the stack before Jacqueline could do so herself.

"You may have it when I am finished," Cynthia said, settling back in her chair and opening the cover.

Jacqueline stuck out her tongue at her younger sister. She might be nineteen years old and learning to look coy and sound alluring, but she was still very much a girl.

Kenneth hadn't noticed Rebecca go upstairs for the tea tray, but when he heard steps coming down from the upper floor, he hurried to open the door for her to pass through easily.

"Thank you," she said stiffly as she passed him.

"It is my pleasure," he said, then wondered if he should have said "You're welcome" instead, or maybe "Might we speak privately for a few moments?" The idea that this meeting was a gift of opportunity he might never have again added a layer of eagerness to what he was already feeling. He felt a bit mad with it.

She set the tea on the table, poured three cups, and then excused herself to assist in the studio.

After twenty minutes, Nancy came into the parlor, and Cynthia took her place in the studio. Rebecca did not make an appearance.

In an attempt to force his thoughts away from Rebecca, Kenneth picked up a periodical of his own. He had not thought that women's fashion would be that interesting, but it was rather fascinating to learn what influenced this ruffle or that cut. For instance, brass buttons had been appearing on women's coats this year, which had apparently been caused by the increased number of men sporting military uniforms at formal events. And the clothing was incredibly complicated.

Much like women themselves, he thought, then remembered he was proving to be a complicated gentleman in his own right.

When Cynthia returned, she pulled the blue-covered periodical from Jacqueline, who had been reading it in her sister's absence. "Your turn," she said, smirking as she settled into a chair.

Jacqueline glared at her as she stood and strode from the room.

Within a few minutes, Nancy began to fidget, so Kenneth played some word games with her and then began drilling her on math problems that could be done without a slate or paper. It was something he'd done with his own sons when they were younger and needed attention and entertainment. He believed mathematics training improved overall intelligence, and Nancy was smart, despite her rambunctious nature.

Rebecca brought a fresh pot of tea and additional biscuits to replenish the diminishing supply. She ignored Kenneth completely.

Kenneth wondered how she'd have interacted with him if this had been their first meeting, but their history made it impossible for him to ever know. If he could have just two minutes to speak with her, perhaps he could put some of his discomfort to rest. Would that also ease her discomfort?

By the time Jacqueline was finished, sighing dramatically as she fanned her face with one hand, Nancy had put her head on the table, napping, Cynthia had started her third periodical, and Kenneth had formulated a plan.

Chapter Twenty-Three

M r. Seffton did not emerge from the studio to bid them farewell, so Kenneth thanked Rebecca, then ushered the girls into the carriage. Once all three of them were seated, he leaned inside while still standing on the street.

"I have some business to take care of in town, so I will not be riding back in the carriage. Please tell Lady Beth that I shall return to Brenning Hall in time for dinner."

"I should love to come with you," Jacqueline said, moving forward on her seat as though preparing to exit the carriage.

"It is not the sort of business that would interest you, I assure you, and as you did not wear walking shoes, I would hate for you to be uncomfortable." He looked away from her to smile at the other girls. "Thank you for being so well-behaved. I am proud to have been your escort. Have a lovely afternoon."

He shut the door before any of them could respond, then stepped back and waved the driver to leave. He could hear the girls squabbling as the carriage jolted forward, and he let out a breath once the horses were at a steady pace.

He turned back to the studio, glancing up and down the street to ensure no one was watching him. He was not dressed as Malcolm, which posed a different sort of risk than going about in disguise. It was a risk he was willing to take in hopes of gaining any measure of absolution for the hurt and embarrassment he'd caused Rebecca.

He knocked on the door and then stepped back. His anxiety rose with every moment he waited for her to open the door.

When the door did open, it was not Rebecca standing there. Instead, it was Mr. Seffton, who had not said a single word to anyone during the appointment.

"What?" the man said with a growl.

"Might I speak with Reb—Mrs. Parker?"

Mr. Seffton slammed the door, making Kenneth flinch slightly. Heat flushed his neck. Rebecca must have told her father what he'd done, and her father hated him for it.

Kenneth liked to think he would defend his children in a similar situation, except his sons would never find themselves in such a situation because they were men who would not be taken advantage of on the side of a road.

What am I to do?

He glanced up and down the street again, at odds with his options. Knock again and risk Mr. Seffton's fist in his nose? Wait for either Mr. Seffton or Rebecca to leave and risk being seen loitering outside of a shop?

A carriage turned the corner, and he dipped his chin to hide his face should the occupants of the carriage be someone he knew.

The carriage drove past, but he stayed where he was, wishing he were dressed as Malcolm and thus enjoying more freedom. But it was important he talk to Rebecca as himself this time. He was so close!

The sound of raised voices pulled him from his thoughts, but he was unsure if the argument was coming from the Seffton house or a different apartment on one side or another. Kenneth stepped closer to the door, leaning in to listen. The yelling was indeed coming from the studio. It was a man's voice, growing louder. A crash sounded from inside, and Kenneth banged his fist on the door.

Everything went silent inside.

He waited a few more seconds then banged on the door again. "Open the door!" he said, trying not to yell.

When no one answered, he took hold of the knob and turned. It wasn't locked.

He stepped inside and saw the shattered plate first. He lifted his eyes and saw Mr. Seffton glaring at him from the other side of the parlor.

Rebecca stood against the wall on the far side, her face red and her chest heaving.

"Rebecca," he said, reaching his hand toward her but still keeping an eye on her father. "Come with me."

She swallowed and looked at the floor, ignoring his hand. "I do not need your help, sir."

He looked toward her, then at the shards of pottery on the

floor. He did not withdraw his hand. "Accept my assistance anyway."

She looked up and held his eyes a moment. He knew her mind was working out what to do. She did not trust him or want his help, but she was also frightened.

"Please," he said quietly.

She swallowed again and then nodded almost imperceptibly. "I need to fetch my things upstairs."

"You are not leaving until I say so!" her father yelled.

"She shall leave as soon as she is ready," Kenneth replied, his words sharp. "This is hardly the way you treat a lady, let alone your daughter."

"Who are you to come into my home and make demands?"

"Mr. Kenneth Winterton, heir to Lord Brenston."

Mr. Seffton's face only reddened. "Get out of my house!" the old man barked.

"I will, as soon as Rebecca is ready to leave with me."

The two men glared at each other.

Kenneth held Mr. Seffton's eyes another moment then waved for Rebecca to leave the room.

She looked at him as she passed him into the hall, and he felt his heart flip in his chest, though he did not look away from Mr. Seffton. He willed her to hurry as she took the stairs to the upper floor. He was feeling dizzy from the confrontation. This was not how he usually went about things.

Rebecca returned quickly with only a small bag, stepping carefully toward the front door.

Kenneth glared once more at her father, then turned without

landing a parting commentary the way he'd have liked to. Had he been the type of man who settled disputes with violence, he very well might have indulged in a solidly placed punch. But he was not that sort of man. He was the sort of man who hid his racing horse from his uncle and kissed women on the side of the road and then lied to avoid conflict.

What an interesting detail of self-assessment to discover just now.

He led Rebecca to the door, then let her pass through first. She was close enough to him that he could smell both paint and cinnamon upon her. Did she paint? Once the door was shut, they walked a short way down the street in silence, leaving the studio behind them.

"I am fine," she said, relieving him of the responsibility of finding something to say. "Thank you."

She began walking away from him. He hesitated only a moment, then hurried to catch up with her. "Where will you go?"

"Home," she said shortly. She paused at the street, checked for carriages, and then hurried across. There were people on the street, trying to hide their notice. He ignored them and stayed right behind her.

"You do not live with your father, then? Do you live at Grangeford?"

She stopped and faced him. "Why are you asking me these questions, Mr. Winterton?" He heard the chill surrounding his name and wondered what it had been like for her to come to terms with who he really was.

"I want to understand your situation," he said. "I want to help if you need help."

"I do not need *your* help." She turned away.

"Does he hurt you?"

"I am not your concern."

"Help me understand, please."

She paused, then turned back to him and stared coldly for a moment before she spoke again. "I have helped in the Grangeford kitchen from time to time. That's why I was there that night. I lived with my father until recently. Though his temper has gotten the better of him, he has not hurt me. I am now in transition to a permanent position in a fine house. Everything *I* told *you* was true, if you are implying otherwise."

He did not miss her inflections. "I was not accusing."

She turned, but he put a hand on her arm. She shook it off and kept walking, forcing him to hurry to keep step with her. A woman sweeping her stoop paused so that she might watch them more closely.

"Rebecca, please," he said, lowering his voice. "Let me explain myself."

She finally stopped again and turned, looking very much as she had the day he'd met her on the road. When her eyes had been green fire and she had lashed him with her sharp tongue.

"Very well, Mr. Winterton. Explain yourself."

He took a few moments to line up the words. This would be his only opportunity. "I sometimes dress as Malcolm so I might feel more freedom within my position and move without restriction." He paused for a breath, but she spoke before he could continue.

"Understood," she said, beginning to turn away.

He took her arm again on instinct, then released it before she could pull away. "No, please let me explain myself, Rebecca. I know I do not deserve it, but please . . . please just listen."

She met his eyes with her chin slightly raised. "You have already explained yourself, Mr. Winterton. All is resolved."

"All is not resolved," he said. "I beg your forgiveness for my actions. It was terribly wrong, and—"

"Women like me expect such treatment from men like you, Mr. Winterton," she said evenly.

Kenneth pulled back in surprise at her words.

"There is nothing unexpected about the discovery, even if I was initially surprised to learn of your lies. I assure you my life has far more important details that deserve my attention, and I shall not lose sleep over you any more than I am sure you have not lost sleep over me. Have a good day, Mr. Winterton."

She left him standing there, helplessly watching her disappear, and feeling smaller than he could ever remember feeling in his life.

Chapter Twenty-Four

Though she had tried to communicate strength and acceptance when Mr. Winterton had tried to explain himself, Rebecca had melted into a puddle of emotion by the time she reached the parsonage.

In some ways, being that close to him, feeling his touch, smelling his scent, was harder than having seen him in the Grangeford dining room the night she'd realized he'd tricked her. Some pathetic part of her wanted to forgive him just so she could stay in his proximity. Adding those unwelcome and inappropriate thoughts to the fear of Father losing his temper again was more than she could manage in a single afternoon. She felt ready to split in half.

"Welcome back," Mrs. Rushford said cheerily from the parlor when Rebecca came through the front door. Her chipper disposition rubbed like needles down Rebecca's spine. "How was the appointment?"

"It went well," Rebecca said stiffly, though her voice quivered. Her head was pounding with thoughts and emotions she could not express to anyone.

"Do come in and sit with me. Tell me all about it. Cook has made the most wonderful strawberry tarts."

Mr. and Mrs. Rushford had been nothing but kind and accommodating to Rebecca. Letting her stay at the parsonage these last weeks and helping to facilitate a repaired relationship with Father, though she felt now that that relationship would never be whole again. However, as much as Rebecca wanted to be a good guest, she was in no shape for company.

"I am afraid I have a pounding headache," Rebecca said, feeling tight in every muscle of her body. "Might we visit later when I've had some time to rest?"

"Of course, dear," Mrs. Rushford said. Then she cocked her head. "Is everything alright?"

Rebecca managed a weak smile through the parlor doorway as she held a hand to her head that was throbbing. "Oh, yes, everything is just as it should be, save my head."

And my heart, she thought as she went up the stairs.

In her room, she wet a cloth from the pitcher in the basin and laid on her bed with the cloth over her eyes while she let the thoughts and feelings surge and wane and tangle and loop in her body and mind.

She'd seen Mr. Winterton in his fancy clothes and arriving in his fancy carriage. He looked so different than Malcolm, and yet he'd *felt* the same. Even though she avoided eye contact and did not engage with him, the awareness of his person was so familiar.

He'd seen Father's treatment of her up close, and though she was humiliated to have a witness and need aid, Mr. Winterton *had* helped her.

She'd been able to speak to him exactly the way she wanted to, strong and sure of herself, just enough edge to her words to set him on his heels. It was fully finished between them now.

The thought made her chin quiver for a moment before she forced the regret deep within her mind. She could never want a man who was so dishonest. Never mind the effect he had upon her.

As for Father . . . she was finished with him too. It hurt her heart in an entirely different way to draw that conclusion, but today had shown her that she was not safe with him. Even when she was not living in the home. Even when she'd come solely to help him. There was nothing left to rebuild, and she wondered how long their relationship had been so inexorably broken. How long had she ignored how poorly he treated her? She felt pathetic and sad.

She did not know how Father would finish the silhouettes for the Brenston granddaughters. He had not done finish work for years. She worried for him, but she would not go back. She could not help him. She could barely help herself.

She closed her eyes beneath the cool cloth, her body full of spinning thoughts and jagged feelings, and tried to sleep.

When she woke, the afternoon light had shifted and the heaviness in her chest was not so weighted. It was a good reminder that darkness never lasted forever. There was always light to be found.

She got up from the bed, repaired her hair, and then headed to the main level. She hoped Cook had not started dinner without her. Helping in the kitchen might improve her mood and help her feel useful.

Tomorrow was her second interview with the Campbells. If all went well, she would begin next week. She was eager to have the new start of a new life even if it was not the life she actually wanted to live. What she wanted was to relive her years with David. A hand at her back when she entered a room, a chest to lay her head upon in the dark, an ear to listen to her talk through her troubles, and a belly to laugh with. It was foolish to think she could have that again, yet she ached to accept that she would not.

Rebecca was on the third stair down when a familiar voice from the parlor brought her up short. She paused, then hurried down the rest of the stairs to the doorway.

"Rose?" she said, looking in surprise at her daughter poised so prettily on the blue settee. Rebecca's eyes shifted to Mrs. Lenning, who was seated to Rose's left, at the same time that Mrs. Rushford spoke.

"Do come in," Mrs. Rushford said, leaning forward and preparing a cup of tea. "I told them you weren't feeling well, but I am so glad you felt up to joining us."

Rebecca entered the room, confused by the unexpected gathering. Rose had been to the parsonage many times, of course; she had visited just last Sunday afternoon. Mrs. Lenning was the bigger surprise, and the two of them together, without any notice, was more surprising still.

Mrs. Rushford chattered about this and that, then handed Rebecca the cup of tea, which was not exactly hot. "Well, I shall excuse myself," she said, standing up. "Have a lovely afternoon."

She quit the room, which left Rebecca on one side of the tea table and Rose and Mrs. Lenning on the other side.

"I am sorry I was not here when you arrived," Rebecca said. "I had a bit of a headache this afternoon."

"Are you feeling better, Mama?" Rose asked, her eyebrows knit together with concern.

"Much," Rebecca said with a smile. "Especially now that I get to see you." She shifted her eyes to Mrs. Lenning. "To what do I owe the pleasure of the visit?"

"Well, I'm afraid is it not entirely social," Mrs. Lenning said, setting down her teacup. "I am here with a proposition."

"A proposition?"

"Or rather, an opportunity," Mrs. Lenning corrected. "We need an upstairs maid at Grangeford. If you recall, I had to let go of one a few weeks ago. We had hoped we could get on without her, but it is not proving to be the case. Rose had mentioned you were considering a position with the Campbells, and I will understand if you still wish to accept that arrangement, but if you were open to it, we would love to have you consider Grangeford."

Rebecca blinked, holding the teacup a few inches above her saucer. "You are offering me a position?"

"Officially, it is a chambermaid," Mrs. Lenning said self-consciously. "But given your earlier service at Grangeford, there would be some additional responsibility, such as helping with dinners and assisting me with the scheduling of the other maids. They are all rather young, and I believe your experience would be a great service to them and to me."

Rebecca returned her cup to the saucer. "I . . . I do not know what to say." She looked at Rose, who was smiling. "I am, of course, flattered by the offer, but Rose and I have spoken of this before, and I feel it would undermine her place to have her mother on staff."

"*I* am on staff," Rose said, raising her chin in that slightly arrogant way she had when she did not want to be questioned.

Rebecca cocked her head and gave her a look. "You are a companion, that is hardly staff."

"I get paid, just as you."

Rebecca turned to Mrs. Lenning. "You understand my hesitation, do you not, Mrs. Lenning? It is unusual enough to have family in positions in the same household, but it is even more unusual to have the daughter in a position above the mother. I do not want to bring any complication to the household, but especially not to Rose."

"But you are considering the offer?" Mrs. Lenning asked, lifting her eyebrows.

Rebecca paused, thinking of how to answer. With both of them looking at her so intently, she could not think of any answer but the truth.

"How could I not consider it?" Rebecca said, setting her cup down on the tea table. "I love Grangeford, and my favorite person in the world is there." She shared a quick look with Rose, but then a thought damped her smile. "Surely the baroness would not approve."

"I spoke with her already," Mrs. Lenning said. "Typically, I make the decisions for general staff, but in this case, I wanted her blessing due to the fact that it *is* a unique situation. She remembered you."

Rebecca narrowed her eyes in disbelief.

"She really did, Mama," Rose said. "She spoke with me after Mrs. Lenning proposed the idea. She is agreeable if the rest of us are."

"What did the Campbells offer you in wages?" Mrs. Lenning asked, getting back to business.

"Five shillings a week, with Wednesday afternoons off and every other Sunday."

Mrs. Lenning nodded. "What were their accommodations?"

"A shared room in the servants' hall," Rebecca said, embarrassed that this was her situation. That she had no home. No place that belonged to her. But she quickly pushed out that thought and invited gratitude in its place. She had much to be grateful for.

"We can offer the same wages and accommodations, except that we do not do every other Sunday off, but every sixth day, whatever day of the week it might land upon. And you shall need to take Thursday afternoons instead of Wednesday to keep the household fully staffed. Will that be acceptable?"

Rebecca nodded, unable to speak for her happiness. She would live in the same household as her daughter again. A place she knew was already safe.

Her mind moved back in time to the night she'd met Malcolm's eyes—*Mr. Winterton's* eyes—across the Grangeford dining table. Her happiness faded.

She would see him again if she served for a dinner party, which Mrs. Lenning had already said would be part of her duties. That would be awful . . . and yet she seemed to cross his path in all manners of ways. To expect she would live out her life in Wakefield without seeing him was silly.

She *would* see him again. And she would manage her reaction to it just as she had managed everything else. In time, she would not react to his presence or wonder how he was. He would become one more nobleman to whom she served fish and cleared plates.

"I would be honored to take the position," Rebecca said, finally finding her words. "Thank you so much."

"Excellent," Mrs. Lenning said, sipping her tea. "I shall sort things out with the Campbells. Can you start on Tuesday?"

"You will sort things with the Campbells?"

"The baroness will pay a token of appreciation. It is standard when one household hires staff from another household."

"But I have not been officially hired at the Campbells."

Mrs. Lenning waved that away. "It is how it is done. Tuesday, then?

Rebecca shared a look with Rose and smiled. This morning had been so uncomfortable with Mr. Winterton and then so frightening with Father, but this afternoon had been remarkable.

"Yes, Mrs. Lenning. Please tell the baroness how much I appreciate this opportunity. Truly, this is a great blessing for me."

Chapter Twenty-Five

This time, Kenneth recognized Rebecca the instant she entered the dining room at Grangeford, a step behind a footman. She kept her eyes down, as did all the staff. He tried not to stare but could not help but track every movement as she set plates in front of each guest.

When she leaned in to set his plate, he took a deep breath, and she paused for a single moment before continuing. He felt sure she knew it was him. He had the mad desire to say hello or touch her arm, but he could not do either. She withdrew and continued serving.

When she was serving directly across from him, she flickered a glance in his direction. Her cheeks pinked, and he felt a ridiculous flutter to know she had noticed him, even though he had no reason to believe she was glad to see him.

It had been nearly three weeks since he'd asked her forgiveness and she'd told him that women like her expected to be treated poorly by men like him. That had cut deeply and stayed with him. He hated being put in that sort of category, but it was true. He *had* treated her badly because it had worked better for him. She was the one who had been hurt by it, even if she tried to act as though it had not made an impact.

Since that day, he had been introduced to another half a dozen women whom Uncle had deemed suitable countesses. They spoke French and tapped his arm with their fans when they laughed. They knew about horses, or so they said, and dressed in the latest fashions. They wore pretty hats and shoes. A few were attractive, and one was very fun to talk to. He was trying to feel something for any of them, but none of them left much of an impression. He needed a countess and could feel his commitment waning to choose a woman with whom he had accord. The process was fatiguing. And if he could not have the sort of marriage he longed for, did it matter who he chose?

He'd also spent that time avoiding Jacqueline, who seemed to show up in the most unexpected places. He had hoped she would lose interest or that perhaps the extra society spurred by his hunt for a wife would introduce some young man to Jacqueline who would be far more interesting than he was. That had not happened, so he continued to dodge her and pretend he did not notice the attention.

Now he was in Rebecca's company once again and felt that something he had felt every other time he'd seen her. The ladies he'd met with their tinkling laughter and well-placed flirtation had no impact compared to her mere presence in the room. He felt it each time she came in, and felt it leave with her upon her withdrawal.

She did not look at him again through the rest of dinner, and it bothered him. The women left for the drawing room, and the men lingered over their port. Though he tried to stay up on the conversations taking place around him, Kenneth could not stop thinking of Rebecca.

Where was she right now? What did she think of him? Was she still angry?

She had shut down his attempts to apologize and made light of his deception. Things did not feel resolved for him. Certainly, he had not said all he wanted to say. Perhaps he could not forget her because his conscience was still not remedied.

He wanted another chance to speak to her but could not think how. When the men left the dining room, Kenneth excused himself by stating he needed to use the facilities—which was true, but not his only intention. A footman pointed him in the right direction, but luckily was not outside when Kenneth finished.

Checking both directions, Kenneth stepped carefully down the hall until he encountered the library. It took a few minutes, but he eventually found what he was looking for: a roll of paper in a drawer and a pencil left upon a shelf near the back of the room. He cut a small piece of paper, scribbled a quick note, then folded the paper into a small square and put it into the pocket of his waistcoat.

He was counting on Rebecca being as aware of him as he was of her so that when she entered the room later, he could drop the note or put it somewhere that Rebecca would see it. There was a great deal of margin for error in his plan, but he was so close to her. Again. And the need to explain himself was pounding upon his ribs like a drum. Again. Surely there was something he could say to relieve his discomfort, and hers.

With the note safely tucked away, he left the room, trying to orientate himself to where he was in the house. He had been here twice now, and he believed the drawing room was . . . to the left. Yes, to the left.

He followed the curvature of the hallway and found himself in a study, which had writing paper and a pen right there on the desk. He could have saved some time had he found this room first, but never mind. He left the study, realizing he'd taken the wrong direction from the library. He went right, but encountered a hallway he did not recognize. He tried to go back but could not find the study.

He stopped and looked around again, recognizing nothing. He turned in each direction, then chose the one that looked the most promising, only to find himself at a dead end. Well, there was a door to the private areas of the house but . . .

He turned back and stared at the door. The private areas of the house meant servants.

Three steps later, Kenneth pushed open the door and was instantly confronted with the smells of braised meat and sweet syrup and the sounds of pots and pans clanging and someone yelling. It was all rather overwhelming, but he took a breath and walked down the stone staircase.

When he appeared at the bottom of the stairs, the yelling

and even the clanking pots fell silent as several heat-reddened faces looked up at him in surprise.

"I am so sorry," he said, feeling his own face heat up at their surprised attention. "I am afraid I got turned around and could not find my way back to the drawing room." He scanned the faces and only just kept from smiling when his eyes met Rebecca's. "You were serving tonight," he said, extending a hand toward her. "Could you help me find my way back?"

"Of course," she said more quickly than he expected, then hurried toward him.

He stepped out of the way, then smiled and nodded at the rest of the servants before he followed Rebecca. The kitchen noises started up again as soon as his back was turned, though the voices were now hot whispers instead of yelling.

Rebecca walked quickly up the stairs. Just before they reached the door, she turned to look at him over her shoulder. Even in the darkened stairwell, he could see the snap of her green eyes.

"Are you mad?" she hissed.

"I really did get lost," he said softly, stepping forward to push open the door for her as a gentleman would. Instead of thanking him or batting her eyelashes, as one of the gentry women might have done, she glared and ducked under his arm. The door shut, and they were three paces down the hall before he spoke again.

"But I also wanted to speak with you." He hurried to step in front of her to prevent her from passing.

"I cannot speak with you," she said in an angry whisper. "I

am a part of the staff here now. If I am seen speaking to you privately—to any guest—I shall be terminated immediately." She stepped to the side, and he stepped as well, blocking her path again.

"I am sorry, Rebecca, but I must have a chance to explain. I shall go mad if I do not resolve this." He felt bad being so aggressive, but not badly enough to stop.

She let out an exasperated sigh. "It is resolved. I have forgiven you."

"But you are still angry, and I am still . . . not at peace. Please, one more chance for us to talk it through, when neither of us are in danger of being seen or needed elsewhere."

"Do you even hear yourself, Mr. Winterton?" she said, still whispering. "You cannot be seen with me as yourself, and I am always needed elsewhere. Let this go. Put it behind you."

"I cannot," he said, putting a hand to his chest. "Not until I feel that I can be fully understood and therefore absolved. Name a time and place, and I shall be there."

She sighed again, looking past him down the hall. "This is ridiculous. We are both going to be missed from where we are supposed to be right now."

"Time and place," he said, biting his tongue to keep from retracting his request and letting her go. He was being a tyrant, and she'd had enough tyranny in her life and from him. Yet he was doing it anyway.

"Alright," she said in surrender. "Eleven o'clock at the walnut tree."

"The walnut tree?" he said. "Is that a pub?"

She bit back a smile as she shook her head. Seeing the curve of her lips lifted him as though he had wings.

"It is an actual tree. Go to the western hedge about a quarter of the way down the drive and follow it south until you reach the tree. It is the largest tree on the property. I can meet you at eleven."

"I will be there." He nodded sharply, beyond thrilled that she'd agreed.

"If you do not come, I will count our connection as finished. I am doing this for you, not me. My conscience is clear."

"You are very lucky to have that," he said, stepping to the side so she could pass him. He fell in step behind her and leaned forward to add, "Thank you for giving me the chance."

"You are ridiculous," she said over her shoulder before leading him through a dark ballroom he swore he had never seen before—a shortcut? Emerging from the other side of the room, he heard voices from the drawing room ahead. He finally recognized the hallway. How had he become so turned around?

She did not pause as she opened the door, and he did not look at her as he passed her in the doorway, and they both snapped into their roles. She closed the door behind him, and Kenneth smiled at a few curious faces that had turned in his direction.

"Where have you been?" Uncle Lester asked from his place in one of the armchairs near the fireplace.

"I'm afraid I became rather turned around," he said, stepping forward to pour himself a glass of scotch. "I ended up in the kitchens, and Rebecca helped me find my way." He turned with his glass in hand to see his uncle shaking his head in irritation at yet another foible on Kenneth's part. The man had no idea.

"Your home is brilliant," Kenneth said to the baroness, lifting his glass to her. "But I think I shall need half a dozen more tours if I am to be expected to find my way without a map."

Chapter Twenty-Six

Kenneth waited until the house was out of sight through the back window of the carriage before tapping on the roof. His uncle and Lady Beth had another social obligation, which left him blessedly alone tonight. The carriage came to a stop, and Kenneth jumped out, his boots crunching on the gravel.

"I will walk home," he said with a half salute, half wave to the driver sitting in the box.

The driver blinked at him. "In the dark?"

"Yes, I feel . . . anxious and am in need of some physical exertion."

The driver's furrowed brow furrowed even more. "In the rain?"

Kenneth hadn't realized it was sprinkling, but they were in Northern England where it rained a great deal of the time. He nodded.

"But it is a chill night."

Gracious, it was rather chilly, wasn't it? Kenneth resisted pulling up the collar of his coat now that he was noticing the temperature, which was quite cool for August. However, he had been in the navy, for goodness' sakes, and he could manage a bit of rain and cold in high-quality boots and the finest coat he'd ever worn.

"I am simply in need of a good stretch of my legs. I assure you, I shall be fine."

"It is near two miles to Brenning Hall by the roads."

Was it that far? Perhaps this was poorly planned, but he'd badgered Rebecca into meeting him. What was a little rain and cold and distance in the dark in comparison with a chance to talk to her again? He nodded confidently at the driver and stepped to the side of the road, walking as though he were going directly home.

The driver clicked the horses to move forward but kept them at a walk as he came even with Kenneth. "Sir, would you like me to wait some distance down the road in case you change your mind?"

That was a good idea, and Kenneth wished he had thought of it, but it would seem haphazard for him to agree now. He needed to portray confidence. If he could not properly manage a conversation with the carriage driver, how was he to have any hope of managing a conversation with Rebecca?

"No, I am fine. Thank you."

The driver kept apace for a few more steps, until Kenneth stopped and turned to face him. "Williams," Kenneth said, summoning the authoritative tone he'd mastered as a lieutenant. "I am a man comfortable with my own company and get very little of it. Please allow me the dignity of walking home by myself, if only to remind myself that I am capable of such independent actions."

The driver's concerned expression remained, but he nodded his head and urged the horses forward.

Kenneth kept walking in the direction of Brenning Hall until he could not hear the carriage, then he turned back the way he'd come and quickened his pace back down the drive.

When he'd left the party, it had been 10:25, and he estimated a solid twenty minutes had passed already. He did not want to be late for the meeting. After how poorly he had treated Rebecca, he did not want to add another offense to the list.

He found the western hedge Rebecca had mentioned and followed it south until he saw the large walnut tree. He sighed in relief. He'd worried she may have made it up in order to send him scampering about the property that had no walnut trees at all.

He wished he had light enough to see his pocket watch so he would know if he were early or late. He ducked beneath the large branches of the tree to get out of the still-drizzling rain and stepped on a walnut, the crack of the shell making him jump. The tree grew beyond the manicured portions of the estate, and it seemed last year's harvest had not been cleared.

He turned to observe the outline of the house, though he could barely see the lit windows through the rain and the shadows, and wondered if Rebecca had been able to get away. He heard another walnut crunch behind him, and, feeling a jolt of anticipation, Kenneth turned in time to be hit in the face with what felt like a rock.

He lifted a hand to his temple only to have another walnut graze his ear. He took a few steps back as he was hit in the shoulder, then the chest.

"Gracious!" he finally exclaimed, bending down to pick up a walnut of his own. He pulled his hand back to throw it, but then realized that his attacker was not a groom looking to protect the property, but a middle-aged woman with blonde hair coming loose from her mobcap. Even in the dark, he could see her angry green eyes. Throwing walnuts gave a clear indication of her mood.

Or at least she *had* been throwing walnuts. Now she stood still, an armful of walnuts held against her chest as she stared at his raised hand. She was not smiling, but he felt a rush of energy all the same to see her. She'd come!

He lowered his hand and let the walnut drop to the ground. "Rebecca," he said. "Thank you for coming."

She was silent another moment, then stepped toward him and began throwing walnuts again.

He was not going to retaliate against a woman, so he ran to the far side of the walnut tree. One walnut hit him as he made his retreat, and another hit the tree moments after he'd taken cover. He pressed his back against the tree trunk and listened carefully to the sound of her steps in order to tell from which side she was approaching. The thrill of having her in his company eclipsed any other reaction he might otherwise have felt.

"You have excellent aim," he said after a few seconds of silence and no walnuts.

"Yes, I do."

Good, she was talking. And she was standing slightly more to his left. He took a step to his right to keep the distance between them as wide as possible. The place where the first walnut had hit him on his right temple still stung, and yet the energy spurring her action meant she cared, which, after their last meeting at her father's house, he had questioned. She was also not bending to his rank or acting in keeping with their societal differences. He liked that very much.

"I appreciate you coming to meet me," Kenneth said from his side of the tree.

"Oh, I am sure you do," she said sarcastically.

"What do you mean by that?"

"You want to apologize again, and I do not want it, again, and yet I have no choice but to come when I am called, do I? Because you are who you are, and I am who I am. Say your piece, then come out so I can pelt you with the rest of these walnuts, and we shall call it settled."

"I do not really want to be pelted with your additional walnuts," Kenneth said. "Is there something I could do or say to dissuade you from that course?"

"No," she said.

She'd moved a fraction closer on the left. He took another step to the right, keeping his back against the tree.

"That is unfortunate," he said.

"For you, perhaps, but not for me. I already feel better, and I still have . . . seven more walnuts in hand."

"You are *still* angry with me, then?"

"Yes, sir."

"For the deception?"

"Yes, sir."

"You do not need to call me 'sir.'"

"Are you telling me what I can and cannot call you, sir?"

"Um, no, you may call me whatever you like if it shall make you feel better."

"Feel better," she repeated in a musing tone. "What would make me feel better would be to finish throwing the walnuts."

"I would really like to come to some other arrangement," Kenneth suggested, turning his head toward her direction and wishing he could see her as they spoke. "Are you sure there is no other point of negotiation?"

"I'm afraid not," she said. "So, you best come out from behind the tree and take your lumps, *sir*."

He considered another moment and then, seeing no other resolution, stepped out from behind the tree. He spread his arms out, giving her as wide a target as he could.

"Then fire away," he said with a nod, careful not to show how much he was enjoying this exchange. He took great satisfaction in the look of surprise on her face.

He had made dinner conversation or parlor talk with so many women since coming to Wakefield, and not one of them intrigued him the way Rebecca did.

She stared at him. He kept his arms out but felt the

playfulness of the mood shift. Though he'd been enjoying their exchange and hoped that some part of her was too, looking at her face reminded him of all the ways he had hurt her. Embarrassed her. Made her life, which already seemed to have a fair amount of difficulty, even more difficult. The levity settled, and the seriousness of his actions occupied the space of his mind.

He dropped his arms to his sides. "I should not have lied to you, Rebecca, but I do not know how I could have told you the truth. Even if that was the right thing to do, it would have hurt and embarrassed you had I'd done so in that moment. Whether that would have caused more or less hurt and embarrassment than what you felt when you *did* realize who I really was, I do not know, but I am deeply sorry for the pain I have caused you.

"Kissing you was an action quite contrary to my nature, but even more contrary to my position, which I am still learning, and I reacted in a way that protected me at your expense. It was self-serving to the extreme, and I am very sorry. I sincerely hope you can forgive me."

She watched him for a few seconds, and he wished he could read her thoughts.

"Why do you care about my forgiveness, Mr. Winterton?" she asked. "I am nothing to you. No one of consequence. There is no need for you to concern yourself over what a common woman thinks of you, so why bother?"

"Because lying to you was wrong," he said simply.

She was silent, and he took the opportunity to look at her with more attention than he had ever been able to do before.

She really was a lovely woman with large eyes and a graceful neck. Her shape showed strength and softness and, despite her maid's uniform and white mobcap, there was something elegant in her posture.

"And," he said, feeling nervous about revealing more but compelled to take full advantage of this moment, "there is something about you that . . . draws my intrigue."

"You are a cad," she said and threw a walnut.

It hit his stomach, but he did not run back behind the tree. "I am a cad because I am intrigued by you?"

"Because you are trying to seduce me after convincing me your motives were moral ones."

"What?" he said, standing up straighter. "I am doing no such thing."

"To you I am a wanton woman who kisses strange men on the side of the road and therefore is likely to agree to a tryst or an arrangement of some sort—am I not? Is that not the basis of your interest all along?"

"Goodness, no," he said, feeling his cheeks heat up. "I am not such a man as that, and I did not for one instant think you were such a woman. I felt we were two lonely people captured by something that surprised us both. I kissed you because I felt you wanted me to."

She snorted and threw another nut. He dodged, and it sailed past his shoulder.

"I was holding the handkerchief to your cheek and bracing the other side of your face with my other hand. You closed your eyes and sighed with such . . . pleasure." The word hung between them, a spot of warmth in the chilly summer night. He noticed her cheeks darken, but she did not throw another walnut, so he took that as permission to continue.

"You took hold of my wrists so I would not pull away, and when I leaned in, you lifted your chin toward me. You *wanted* me to kiss you, and not because you were a wanton woman, but because you were lonely, as was I. I believed it had been a very long time since you had been that close to a man, just as it had been a very long time since I had been that close to a woman.

"I have plenty of flaws, Rebecca, and you have had a front seat to several of them in the few opportunities when our paths have crossed, but I am not a man that would take advantage. If I had not believed you wanted to be kissed as much as I wanted to kiss you, I would have contained my desire."

The silence that followed his words was fraught with an emotion he could not identify as she processed his words.

"So it is my fault you kissed me," she said.

His heart seized, and he shook his head immediately. "That is not what I meant at all, and if I suggested as much, I apologize. If I misinterpreted your feelings that day, I apologize even more."

"You are apologizing for the kiss then."

He thought back to the moment on the side of the road, after the kiss when he'd thought that apologizing would be the gentlemanly thing to do. He clearly saw her face as she had smiled up at him following the kiss, eyes bright, cheeks pink.

"No, actually, I do not apologize for the kiss. It was invigorating, and I stand by my opinion that it was something we shared, neither taken nor forced. I apologize for my lies that followed, but I shall keep the memory of the kiss and your participation in it. I have plenty of regrets in my life, but that kiss is not one of them."

She blinked, then selected a walnut and pulled her arm back.

He closed his eyes tightly, preparing for impact and hoping she would not hit him in the face again. The walnut hit the ground behind him. Three more walnuts similarly missed him before he dared open his eyes. He held her gaze as she threw the final walnut without bothering to aim. He already knew she could hit him if she wished to.

Rebecca let out a breath and brushed her hands clean. "Very good," she said. "Consider all forgiven."

He was standing between her and the house quite by accident but realized his good fortune when she began to walk toward the house, coming within a few feet of him.

"Rebecca," he said in a quiet voice before she passed him completely, "can we talk some more?"

She stopped, standing nearly shoulder to shoulder, but separated by several feet. She turned to face him, and he did the same. "What on earth would we talk about?"

"I have no idea," he said. Being this close to her filled him with energy. "But I would love for us to think of something. We had a range of topics that day in Grover Park."

She raised her eyebrows. "You mean when you told me about your sons and the discomfort of your position as the heir's *valet*? Do you even have sons?"

"Yes," he said, nodding. He struggled not to reach out and touch her arm. She was so close. "Everything I told you was the truth except my identity."

"Your identity as the heir's valet from Manchester, who was one of Mr. Winterton's seamen back when he was a lieutenant in the king's navy? Except that wasn't your story, it was Malcolm's."

"Yes, Malcolm, who has no sons and is quite content in his place, as opposed to myself, who continues to struggle with the change in station and the new expectations set upon me. As strange as it sounds, I was more honest with you than I have been with anyone else since I came here, except Malcolm, I suppose."

She faced the house, putting her profile in silhouette against the night sky, which made him think of her father's work and the depth of her story that he did not know.

"Are you sorry for the kiss, Rebecca?"

She turned back to him, and for several seconds, they held each other's eyes. "I am not sorry for the kiss," she finally said as soft as the moonlight. "Only that you are not actually a valet."

She walked toward the house again, and he hurried to catch up with her.

"What do you mean by that?" He thought he knew, but he wanted to be sure.

She stopped and faced him, cocking her head slightly. "You know nothing about me, Mr. Winterton, or my life and situation."

He opened his mouth, prepared to list the things he did know. He knew she had a daughter who served as the baroness's companion, that she had lost her husband, had a cruel father, worked hard, and was smart and self-possessed. He knew she had lived in Wakefield all her life, she knew how to speak her mind, and she was an excellent kisser.

"You *think* you know," she said, startling him at how closely she had read the direction of his thoughts. "But you cannot know me because you cannot possibly know what it is to make your way in a world that gives you very few opportunities.

"On the day we met upon the roadside, I had decided on a course that would give me security, but nothing more. Many women in my place would be lucky to have even that much. After meeting you—or rather, after meeting Malcolm . . ." She paused and looked away from him.

He noticed her cheeks were flushed and imagined she was questioning her decision to be so frank with him.

"Tell me," he said, taking half a step closer.

She let out a breath and reached up to tuck a lock of hair into her cap before she met his eyes. "After meeting you, I realized I was capable of feeling more than I thought I was. I realized that to saddle myself to a man who did not spark such feelings would never satisfy me now that I knew what was possible. I began a journey toward a different sort of security and safety. I began to consider a different life."

"With me?" he said, then shook his head, understanding what she meant. "No, with *Malcolm*, who was within your . . . reach."

She laughed without humor. "I am not quite that naïve. But

the feelings I felt were proof that I could still feel them. And if I could feel them with you, then I could feel them with another."

"Then why did it matter that I was a valet and not the heir?"

She met his eye again and held it a moment. "Because a valet might have seen possibility in me. I could only ever have been a dalliance for the heir to the earldom."

"Rebecca," he said with a gasp as though he'd been hit in the stomach. "It was not like that. I felt something, I . . . still feel something with you. For you . . . I—"

"Stop," she said, smiling slightly and shaking her head. "Even if that is true, it is also impossible. At least within the bounds of decency, which you claim to adhere to."

He wanted to argue, but the look of resignation on her face convinced him to hold his tongue. He swallowed the paltry argument that would do neither of them any good and looked away from her eyes, only to have his gaze settle on her lips. He felt the same flip of his stomach he'd felt that day on the road.

"It *is* impossible, Mr. Winterton."

He continued to stare at her perfect lips. Bow-shaped. Pink. Soft. "You already said that." He looked into her eyes.

Her expression had changed, and he recognized the same energy of invitation he'd felt the first time they'd met. He took a step forward to show his intention, then stopped. "You can continue to the house, Rebecca. I will not pursue you. However, if you wanted to stay I would not prevent it."

She stayed where she was and took a deep breath.

"It is *impossible*," she said without moving away.

He took another step toward her, not looking away from those green eyes.

She did not retreat from his approach.

"What if, for five minutes, it *was* possible?" he said, his blood turning hot in the chill night. The rain may have increased, he could not tell. "Possible to feel again what we felt that day—if only to remind us both that it is something we are capable of."

She watched him another moment, then took the final step to close the space between them.

He took her face in his hands, and when her lips met his, he let go in order to wrap his arms around her and pull her to his chest, answering her wanting with his own. She had said she expected to find a man of her station with whom she could feel this way, but for now, she was in his arms, and she knew exactly who he was. There was nothing unsettled between them, and, in that, they stood on equal ground. He would not take that for granted for a single moment.

Chapter Twenty-Seven

Rebecca picked up the list from Mrs. Lenning's desk, reading it over as she walked through the kitchen.

Black thread

Liniment oil

Paraffin

Pick up the baroness's order from the glover

She had been at Grangeford for more than a month now. Managing the other maids had come easy to her, and the other girls respected her position despite her being the newest staff member. She was several years older than any of them, which surely made a difference, and she could read and write, which many of them could not. Mrs. Lenning had given her extra responsibilities, such as picking up a few items from town today. It felt good to be trusted and to know she was doing well in her position.

"Is there anything you need, Mrs. Tarpin?" Rebecca asked

the cook as she tied on her straw bonnet. Rose had been planning to join her, but at the last minute had been invited to attend a luncheon with the baroness. Rebecca did not mind the solitude for an hour. She saw Rose every day, and that was magical.

The cook sighed dramatically. The woman always acted as though she were under a great deal of duress, but Rebecca was getting used to the woman's moods and thought they might actually count one another as friends one day.

"Black peppercorns," Mrs. Tarpin said after a moment. "That fool girl of mine spilled the last packet this morning."

"I shall fetch some, then," Rebecca said. "I'll be back by three o'clock."

Mrs. Tarpin nodded, then turned back to the duck she was dressing for dinner.

Rebecca followed the path that cut behind the stables, taking her time and enjoying the clear autumn day. The gold leaves were beginning to turn, and in another week or so, the orange leaves would join. By the time the reds burst on to the scene, most of the golden leaves she saw now would carpet the path she was walking on. The seasons turned quickly in Yorkshire, and she made sure to enjoy each one.

She was happy at Grangeford, trusted and appreciated. She shared a room with Debra, the next most senior maid, and they got on well.

She had heard nothing from Father, which caused some heartache from time to time, but she had also not realized how difficult it had been to live with him until she hadn't been there anymore. She hoped one day to resolve things enough that they could feel like family again, but she was willing to wait for that to happen.

She took a deep breath when she passed a wild rose bush, inhaling the fragrance and letting it add to the beauty of the day.

The path exited the woods near the foundry, and she followed High Street into the market district of Wakefield. She found the liniment and paraffin at the apothecary, the black peppercorns at the grocer, and crossed the street in order to go to the notion shop for the thread.

"Mrs. Parker?"

Rebecca turned around and smiled politely at Miss Cynthia Marlow, the middle Brenston granddaughter, a slight shiver running through her at even the slightest connection to Kenneth.

Though it had been more than a week since their kiss beneath the walnut tree, she'd thought of nothing else in the moments when work did not demand all of her focus.

What the second encounter lacked in energy compared to the first kiss, it more than made up for in length and diligent attention. She'd been soaked to the skin by the time she'd returned to the house that night, yet was as warm as though she'd spent an hour before the fire, which she had done in order to be dry before she made her way to her room.

Would Miss Cynthia tell him they'd crossed paths in town? What would he say?

"Miss Cynthia," Rebecca said, giving a curtsey and focusing her attention. "Good afternoon."

"Good afternoon to you," Miss Cynthia said in return.

"Thank you," Rebecca said just as two people stepped out of the doorway behind Miss Cynthia.

Mr. Winterton smiled at her, and additional details of their last meeting enhanced the memory she'd already been entertaining. The rain upon their faces . . . his arms around her . . . his mouth on hers. The memory did not embarrass her as she'd expected it might. Instead, she smiled easily and held his eyes a moment longer than necessary before she curtseyed to him as well.

"Good afternoon, Mr. Winterton," she said.

"Good afternoon, Mrs. Parker. How are you?"

It was too personal a question to ask of someone below his station, but she did not mind. In fact, she chose to believe he meant it rather than simply asking out of good manners.

The sound of someone clearing a throat reminded her that Mr. Winterton was not alone; she'd quite ignored that fact, focusing instead on the pleasure of seeing him. She turned her gaze and dropped yet another curtsey to Miss Jacqueline Marlow, who clung to Mr. Winterton's arm.

"Miss Marlow," Rebecca said. "Good day."

"Thank you," Miss Marlow replied.

"We were, um, picking up some bonnets for the girls," Mr. Winterton said, holding up a hatbox.

"For a garden party next week," Jacqueline added.

Rebecca looked past him to the shop they had just exited, which was, in fact, a milliner's shop. Two shops past them was the notion shop that would have the thread for Mrs. Lenning's list.

"I am sure the bonnets are lovely," Rebecca said, smiling at the girls as she made to step around them. "Wonderful to see you."

"When shall our silhouettes be finished?" Jacqueline asked.

Rebecca shared a quick look with Mr. Winterton before focusing her attention on Jacqueline. "Have you not received them?"

"No," Jacqueline said, shaking her head. "Mama sent a note two weeks ago requesting an update but heard nothing back."

"I am sorry to hear that," Rebecca said, both surprised and yet not surprised. Father had not been doing his own finishing work for years. But she had also not spent a great deal of time worrying about it as there were so many other things to be attentive too. "I'm afraid I am no longer assisting my father in his work."

She felt some concern settle upon her as worry for Father entered in. Just earlier today she'd felt so good about the changes in her life.

"You were assisting him at the time we had our sittings," Jacqueline said, her tone a bit sharper than it had been to this point. "Surely there is some responsibility there."

"That is enough," Mr. Winterton said, though gently. "I shall enquire with Mr. Seffton myself. I had not been informed of the delay but will find out what the expectation is."

"She can follow up more easily than you can, Mr. Winterton. We've the Taylors' dinner to prepare for tonight."

Mr. Winterton looked at Rebecca, in fact she was not sure he had looked away. "I shall follow up," he said again. "Are you well, Mrs. Parker?"

Jacqueline made a slight scoffing noise in her throat. Everyone ignored it.

"I am well, Mr. Winterton."

"I am glad to hear that."

She could hear the softness in his voice and could sense the rising curiosity of the Marlow sisters. She looked away, ducked her head, and stepped around the party, hiding the smile that might be misinterpreted. Or worse, properly interpreted. *It is impossible*, she told herself. But it was also nice to know that he thought well of her. Nice to remember the moments they had shared. Nice to know he had wanted those kisses as much as she had.

"Good day," she said, her eyes on the nearby notion shop as she successfully navigated past them, too far from Mr. Winterton to brush against his coat, though she was sorely tempted.

She was several steps away when she felt a touch on her arm. She knew it was him before she turned. The smile that came to her lips was easy and sincere.

"I just wanted to say how nice it is to see you," he said quietly.

"It is nice to see you as well, Mr. Winterton."

"Really?"

The sincerity in his tone was so endearing. "Really," she said.

"I am very glad we can . . . talk. Be friends."

Friends?

They could not be friends, and the realization made her sad, but she refused to let her thoughts linger over it. It felt better to be grateful that they could both think well of one another rather than feel rancor or contention. It could not be more, but it could be *this*.

"As am I, Mr. Winterton," she said, then lowered her voice another level. "And I thank you for speaking with my father. I have not seen or heard from him since . . . that day."

"It is not your responsibility; I am glad to help resolve it."

She did not like feeling that she needed him to take care of her, and yet she was not ready to interact with her father again. "Thank you."

"Of course," he said, then looked over his shoulder, presumably at the two young women waiting for his escort. "I wish we could keep talking."

"We cannot," she said, standing straighter as a woman passed them and looked at them in such a way that Rebecca knew their differences in station were being noted.

"I know."

They held each other's eyes a moment, and he began to turn away.

"Mr. Winterton?"

The eagerness in his expression when he turned back was invigorating. "Yes?"

"Might you do me a favor and let me know how my father is getting on when you speak with him? I worry about him, and I worry about his work."

"I shall absolutely inform you of our meeting . . . somehow."

Yes, somehow.

"Thank you," she said.

He nodded, then bowed slightly to her and returned to his companions. She watched them walk toward the Brenston carriage, complete with the family crest painted on each door.

Chapter Twenty-Eight

It was too early for a social call, but Kenneth had to be back to Brenning Hall in time for morning visits, and this call was not a social one.

The Brenston carriage dropped him off in front of the Seffton studio and then parked around the corner to wait until Kenneth finished his errand. The street was too narrow for the carriage to wait out front.

Kenneth was anxious but also eager to fulfill his promise. Resolving the situation of the undelivered silhouettes would have two benefits—it would relieve Lady Beth's frustration and it would allow him to interact with Rebecca at least one more time. The latter motivation was certainly the stronger of the two.

Kenneth knocked lightly on the front door, then stepped back to observe the house. He saw the curtain on the second level move. Mr. Seffton was home. Good.

He waited long enough that Mr. Seffton could have had

time to answer the door, but when the door remained shut, he knocked again, a bit louder this time.

After another minute of standing outside a closed door, he knocked louder still. He was going to draw the attention of curious neighbors soon, but he steeled himself against their notice. He had every right to be here.

Also, in his most optimistic fantasies, when he met with Rebecca to explain how he had resolved the situation, it would end with them kissing. Again. Such imagined receptions could give a man a great deal of motivation.

The next time he knocked, he banged his knuckles on the door eight distinct times before he finally felt the reverberation of someone coming down the stairs.

He was ready when the old man pulled the door open. "What do you want?"

Kenneth had gotten used to people treating him with deference; Mr. Seffton's brusque manner surprised him, but only for a moment.

"I am Kenneth Winterton, nephew of the earl of Brenston. I am here to resolve the situation regarding the silhouettes of the Brenston granddaughters."

The direct answer brought Mr. Seffton up short. He'd apparently counted on his powers of intimidation the same way Kenneth had expected his dress and position to control this exchange.

"What?" Mr. Seffton said.

Kenneth was getting better at acting his place, but it did not mean that his heart was not thundering in his chest. He had never been one for confrontation, even when serving in the navy, and had been much more comfortable as simply a gentleman living a gentleman's life.

"The Brenston granddaughters' silhouettes were expected weeks ago, and our attempts to garner an update have gone unanswered. I am here for an answer as to when we can expect them."

Mr. Seffton snorted and attempted to close the door, but Kenneth stepped forward and put his palm out, pushing the door open and stepping into the foyer. He was several inches taller than the old man and at least two decades younger.

"Get out of my house!" the old man barked, his red eyes narrowed. The distinct smell of gin wrapped around him like a shroud. Was that the issue? Was Rebecca's father a drunkard?

"Show me the silhouettes," Kenneth said, staring the old man down. "Or return the deposit we have already paid."

"I shall call the constable!"

"Good," Kenneth said, folding his arms over his chest. "I shall tell him how we paid a decent price upon our sitting yet have seen no results."

Mr. Seffton continued to scowl. "I shall complete them when I have the time. Now get out of my house."

Kenneth held the man's eyes a bit longer and then strode past him toward the studio. The room was set up exactly as it had been when he'd come with the girls all those weeks ago. He walked to the heavy drapes covering the windows and pulled them open, sending a dance of dust into the air.

"It seems you have not had a sitting in some time," he said.

"Get out!" Mr. Seffton pointed toward the front of the house.

Kenneth thought of how his uncle would react in such a situation and pulled himself up straighter, lifting his chin and squaring his shoulders as he looked about the room.

When they had been at the studio on the day of the sittings, he had watched Rebecca roll the drawings of each girl together and tie each roll with string. A quick survey of the room revealed three such scrolls in the corner.

He walked over and picked up one of the rolls. Along the top was written *Cynthia Brenston, July 12, 1819*. A quick inspection revealed the other two rolls were those of Nancy and Jacqueline. He turned back to Mr. Seffton.

"You have done nothing?"

And then, in an instant, Kenneth thought he understood. Rebecca had been her father's assistant, but she had left that day and never returned, so the work had not been done. Clients saw Mr. Seffton working during the sitting, and then saw the final result, which Kenneth remembered from the silhouette he had seen at the Langley house. But they never saw the true talent behind the art. *Rebecca* was the key.

"Get out!" Mr. Seffton said again, his hand shaking as he pointed toward the door.

Kenneth had a new idea—a better one. He picked up all three scrolls and glared at the old man. "We are settled. You may keep the deposit. I shall take the sketches."

Mr. Seffton grunted and shook his head. "For all the good they will do you."

"Far more than they are doing you, Mr. Seffton. Good day."

He walked past the old man to the front of the studio, let himself out of the house, and then stood on the street with three rolls of sketched silhouettes in his arms, trying to determine what his next step should be.

Chapter Twenty-Nine

R ebecca?"

She looked up from the bed she was making. One of the guest rooms had its linens changed every third Monday to ensure they were freshly made in case of unexpected guests.

"Yes, Maude, what do you need?"

"There is a man here for you. At the kitchen door."

Rebecca straightened, instantly thinking it must be Mr. Winterton, and then quickly amending that idea because of course it could not be him. "I shall be right there. Thank you."

She balled up the three-week-old linens and put them in the basket for the laundress. She then tried to pretend she did not see the curious glances of the staff as she passed by them. Working at Grangeford was fulfilling, but she did miss her privacy.

She let herself out the kitchen door, closing it behind her

while still feeling eyes watching her through the kitchen windows.

The man had his back to her as she crossed the small yard. It was the sight of a familiar coat that stopped her.

The man turned and smiled nervously. "Mrs. Parker," he said.

"Malcolm," she said in return, then swallowed. He was tall and thin and . . . not Mr. Winterton.

He looked surprised that she knew him, but then glanced at his coat and seemed to understand. He closed the distance between them, though he did not come too close, and lowered his voice. "I have something for you." He passed a folded paper to her.

She took it and, keeping her back to the audience in the kitchen, opened the message.

> *Dear Rebecca,*
>
> *In my attempt to sort things with your father, I have ended up in possession of three scrolls that I believe are the sketches he made of the Brenston granddaughters. I am unsure what to do with them, but I believe you know precisely the next steps.*
>
> *I am equally unsure how to communicate with you, but Malcolm can be trusted by both of us. Please advise me on how to move forward.*
>
> *I hope you are well.*
>
> *Yours truly,*
> *Kenneth B. Winterton*

The real Malcolm cleared his throat. "He asked me to bring back your reply," he said.

"Yes," Rebecca said. "Let me think for a moment." She glanced back toward the house and saw at least three faces disappear from where they had been watching. She faced Malcolm and realized that she essentially had two choices—one would allow her to see Mr. Winterton again and the other would not. She gave herself a few seconds to consider the options, then chose the one she should not have chosen.

"Tell him I am able to finish the work if that is what he would like. I shall need a space to work and some supplies. If he managed to get the sketches from my father, perhaps he could get the other things I need as well."

Malcolm was not smiling as he searched his pockets while shaking his head. "You are as bad as he is."

She felt the accusation run through her like a spark set to dried-out summer grass. "What do you mean by that?"

He held her eyes as he found the stub of a pencil and took back the letter she'd just read. "I think you know precisely what I mean. There are any number of artists you could choose to finish the work, you know that as well as he does." He sighed, then folded the note and turned it so he had a blank surface upon which to write. "What supplies do you need, and when would you have the time to do the work?"

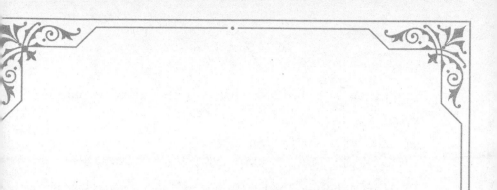

Chapter Thirty

Rebecca arrived at the Brenston dowager cottage just after six o'clock in the morning on her day off, which happened to be a Tuesday. It felt cold enough that Rebecca would not have been surprised to see frost on the ground, but it was only September, and frost was several weeks away yet. The sun was not yet up, but the birds were triumphing the morning as she let herself in through the unlocked kitchen door.

"Good morning," she said, pausing to listen for evidence of anyone else being in the house. Malcolm had ferried a series of notes between Kenneth and Rebecca to solidify these arrangements. The last note had said she'd be alone and that all would be ready for her. The silence that echoed through the cottage confirmed that to be true.

She felt both disappointed and relieved that Mr. Winterton was not there. She had no idea how to interact with him. Were they friends, as he had said when they had last spoken on the street? Was that possible? Should it be?

It cannot be, she decided.

At least his absence afforded her the solitude she needed to finish the cutouts for the Brenston granddaughters and save her father's reputation.

Rebecca rolled out the first sketch on the massive table in the cottage, enjoying the thrill of creation she had missed these past weeks. She used two paperweights and two stones to hold down the corners of Miss Cynthia's upper body sketch and smoothed the paper that still wanted to roll.

Using the tools Mr. Winterton had somehow retrieved from Father's studio, she created a grid of four-inch squares on the sketch, and two-inch squares on a smaller and thicker paper using the framing square—a metal ruler in the shape of an L. Reducing the sketch to half-size was then done by transferring the exact lines that filled each four-inch square to the corresponding two-inch square. It involved mathematics, a steady hand, and complete focus, yet she felt herself relax into the process as though it were a well-loved pair of house slippers.

She was halfway through the transfer when she heard a door open behind her. She smiled to herself and continued to transpose the image—square by square—while listening to his footsteps draw closer.

"Good morning, Mrs. Parker," his voice said, the sound of it moving through her like the vibrations of a thunderstorm. The thrill would pass as these moments they stole were only moments, but, like those summer storms that came and went, and the finish work on these silhouettes, she would enjoy these moments while they lasted.

She did not face him, enjoying the delicious suspense of it all. "Good morning, Mr. Winterton," she said while continuing her work. "You have furnished me quite the studio."

"Do you like it?"

She finally turned to look at him over her shoulder, matching his smile with one of her own. "Very much. Dare I ask how much trouble it was to arrange?"

"Do you enjoy seeing a grown man cry?"

His smile grew, and she laughed while turning back to the work laid out in front of her.

"It was not so much trouble," he said, coming farther into the room. "The cottage is awaiting workmen next week, and your father was more accommodating than expected."

"Dare I ask how much that accommodation cost you?"

"I paid the remainder of the bill," Mr. Winterton said after a moment.

Rebecca was embarrassed that her father had asked such a price for having done only the sketches, and also touched that Mr. Winterton would do it for the sake of everyone involved. "I am sorry."

"Don't be," he said, holding her gaze until she looked back to her work. He came around the table, studying the two images—one full-sized, one reduced. "Is that how it is done?"

Rebecca nodded. "This shall become my pattern," she said as she finished one square on the reduced pattern and moved to the next. "I shall cut out the pattern, then transfer it to the black weave, which will also be cut and set upon the white background." She waved her hand toward the black paper stored on the sideboard of the empty dining room.

"Fascinating," he said. "How long have you been doing your father's work?"

She was quiet for a few moments. She'd never revealed her contribution to anyone, not even Rose. It felt like a betrayal to tell, but a betrayal for whom? Father? Rose? Herself? "I have always helped with the finish work, but I began to do all of it when Rose and I moved into my father's home some eight years ago."

"His decision or yours?"

She considered the question while she transferred two more squares. "Mine, actually." She'd never said that out loud either. "I could not do the sketching—people would never trust a woman artist—but I could do the rest without anyone knowing. I suggested to Father that my assisting him would compensate for him housing us, and the responsibility became mine."

"Yet it is your father's signature on each piece."

She looked up at him, pencil poised above the paper. "You have seen my father's work?"

"I believe it was *your* work—Mary Langley's shade that hangs at the top of her stairs."

Rebecca nodded and went back to the transfer. "Father was the one hired, and his is the hand that did the sketch."

"And you did everything else. Hardly seems like a fair distinction that it belongs only to him."

"There is a great deal of unfairness in the world," she said, keeping her eyes on her work. "Yet I was able to do something I love." She waved her hand over the table of sketches. "That has been luxurious."

"Luxurious," he repeated, then fell silent, watching Rebecca finish the transcription of the upper sketch. He helped her roll up the original, then set the pattern aside on an empty sideboard and unrolled the next full-sized scroll. Nancy's. He settled himself in a chair and watched in silence for several minutes.

"I have never had anyone watch me work before," Rebecca said when she could not stand being so close to him and not interacting.

"That is unfortunate," he said, shifting in his chair. "It is fascinating."

She laughed. "It is not."

"Then perhaps it is *you* that is fascinating."

"That is most assuredly *not* true," Rebecca said, shaking her head as though that might cool the heat in her cheeks. "I am as ordinary as a woman could be."

"Is that what you believe?"

She looked at him again, and for the first time wondered at the propriety of being in a house with him, alone, where no one knew where they were. Were she a woman of his class, this would be considered a compromising situation between them. Yet here they were, him seated in a holland-covered chair wearing a coat that likely cost a year's worth of her wages. He leaned closer to the table, focused on her work. How was it that their paths continued to cross in so many ways? What was she to make of it?

"I sketch," he said, pulling her attention back to him.

"You do?"

He nodded self-consciously, not meeting her eye. "Buildings mostly, but some other things as well."

"I would love to see your work."

He shook his head before she finished her comment. "It is generally frowned upon for a man to draw. It is a decidedly feminine pursuit."

Rebecca laughed. "My father makes his living from *drawing*. He is quite respected for it."

"Oh, well, I suppose it is a . . . class circumstance."

"Ah, as so many things tend to be." She focused more intently on her work, the reminder of all that separated them thick in the air.

She finished the pattern and set it with the other, then began on the third. They talked more, about Wakefield and Sussex and horses and art and then nothing at all. It was lovely silence.

He watched.

She worked.

When the third pattern was finished, she began to cut slowly and carefully so as not to lose any of the detail.

A clock from somewhere deeper in the dowager cottage chimed 10:00.

Mr. Winterton stood from his chair. "I wish I could stay all day."

"It is better that you go," she said, keeping her words soft in hopes of not sounding as rude as she might otherwise. "I shall not make for very good company as this shall take the majority of my attention."

"How much do you think you will be able to finish today?"

"I shall have all the black-weave cutouts finished by day's end," Rebecca said. "I can return on Thursday afternoon and should be able to complete the mounting then."

"I shall be in Castleford that day," Mr. Winterton said, sounding disappointed. "There is a livestock show where my uncle has been asked to present the prizes."

"That is probably for the best," Rebecca said, not looking at him.

"Do you think so?"

She nodded.

He came to within a few feet of her, and her awareness began to buzz. "Thank you for doing this, Rebecca."

"You are welcome, Mr. Winterton."

"Would you please call me Kenneth?"

She stopped her work and stood straight, her back aching from having been bent over the table for so long. She looked at him, then shook her head slowly. "I think it best that I do not."

He took another step toward her, and she should have stopped him, but she didn't. His hand touched her arm, then trailed up to her shoulder. He ran his fingers from the back of her neck to her collarbone.

She had decided before today that she would not kiss him again—that part of their relationship needed to be finished—but when he took a step closer, she took a step toward him as

well. She set down the penknife so she could put her full intention into this.

Their hands and mouths knew just where to go and what
to do. It was so incredibly simple for this part between them to
work. Was it the forbidden fruit of it all? Was it the secrecy? Or
was it, as Kenneth had suggested, their individual loneliness that
enriched the physical exchange?

She did not know and could not make herself care. Moments
came and went, but moments made a life. If this was to be their
last kiss, then she did not want to miss a single moment.

Chapter Thirty-One

It was another dinner party at Grangeford, but the first one since the completed silhouettes had been left on the dining room table of the dowager cottage, ready to be taken to the frame-maker for the final presentation. Rebecca had not left a note—just the beautifully crafted pieces that Kenneth would see every day for the rest of his life in the parlor of Brenning Hall. They had been completed with the same signature found on the full-sized silhouette of Mary Langley, but only Kenneth knew that Rebecca had signed her father's name.

Lady Beth had oohed and aahed over Mr. Seffton's work, and Kenneth had thought about how unfair it was. As Rebecca had said, however, there was a great deal of unfairness in the world. For instance, he was a guest at the baroness's table, and there were two women in attendance for the intent purpose of him evaluating their potential to be the future Countess Brenston. But Rebecca was serving, which meant he was tracking her every movement while trying, and failing, to be attentive to his dinner companions on either side.

He'd seen Rebecca three times during dinner and had kept a sharp eye on the door each time she was not in the room. Their last few meetings had been . . . healing, for lack of another word, and seeing her again left him energized. He deliberately ignored the fact that when he returned to his tower room, he would toss and turn with the turmoil of what lay between them.

When Rebecca entered the drawing room with the playing cards the baroness had requested—his fourth chance to see her this evening—she tucked a tiny slip of paper beneath the edge of a vase on her way out. She'd known he was watching. He liked that.

When Kenneth could do so without drawing attention, he moved to the vase and casually slid the note into his sleeve. Later, he stepped outside on the veranda to get some air and opened the note. It held an invitation.

Walnut tree at 11:00?

He rubbed the paper between his thumb and finger, then tucked it into the inside pocket of his coat. He should not go, but of course he would. The evening was all the better for having Rebecca to look forward to.

He returned to the guests and continued talking to the women he now found even less interesting. He watched the minute hand on the clock move forward, willing it to move faster.

Kenneth had arrived to the party in the same carriage as Uncle Lester and Lady Beth, which made it more complicated to slip away unnoticed. Uncle Lester was enjoying the card play and would argue with Kenneth's early departure, so Kenneth left a message with a footman that he was walking home.

It was completely against class and character for him to do such a thing, but he did it anyway, not caring that it would lead to a row with his uncle in the morning. Not caring that the other guests would think him ill-mannered.

All he cared about was seeing Rebecca.

They met beneath the walnut tree at eleven. It was not raining, but it was quite cold; it was closer to fall than summer now.

"You received my note," she said as she approached him, a heavy shawl about her shoulders.

He smiled at her in the darkness, feeling the former tension of the evening—the burden of having to say the right things to the right people in the right way—shift, lifting like a weight from his back.

He removed his cape and settled it upon Rebecca's shoulders.

"Oh, no," she said, attempting to refuse it. "You'll be chill."

He did not allow the argument and buttoned it beneath her chin, resisting—only just—kissing her right at that moment. "I'll be fine," he said, extending his arm. "A walk?"

She put her arm through his, and they walked and they talked and they laughed, finding new ways in which their stories intertwined. Both parents. Both having lost their partners. Both having chipped away a life from the stone they felt stuck in.

"The last time we met at this tree, you said you had been

considering a marriage proposal," Kenneth said when they had looped back to the tree. It had been nearly an hour of uninterrupted conversation. He wasn't sure how she'd managed to get away from her duties at the house, but he knew he could not keep her for much longer.

"I did not yet have a proposal. But I think Mr. Timoltson would have asked if I had encouraged him," she said, leaning into him slightly.

Did she notice that was her habit when she was talking about something personal? He liked that she felt so comfortable with him.

He glanced at her, searching her face for regret. He did not see any but wondered if that was because he did not want to.

"I am comfortable here," she said, looking toward the house through the trees. "I see Rose every day, and I get on with the staff. The baroness is a kind and generous employer."

She let go of his arm and turned to face him as she undid the cape fastened at her neck. He wished he could let her keep it, but that was impossible. Instead, he took it back and held it over his arm as the warmth it had absorbed began to fade like their time together.

"I am glad we can still be friends, Mr. Winterton. I have enjoyed our time together and will always be grateful for it."

"Kenneth."

"Mr. Winterton," she repeated. She stepped away from him instead of toward him, but she held his gaze as she did so. Her point could not have been clearer—she was leaving. This would be their last meeting.

"It is like that, then?" he said.

"It is," she repeated. "We have always known it."

There were so many things he wanted to say—that it shouldn't be this way, that he could not imagine feeling this comfortable with someone else—but saying anything would change nothing.

He felt the first drop of rain and stepped toward her, aching for one last kiss.

She took another step back and shook her head. "That will only make it harder to say goodbye. This final encounter between us will not end in a kiss, just well-wishes for your future."

She might think she was protecting their hearts by not sharing a kiss, but he knew better. The intimacy of their conversation was more profound than the intimacy of a kiss. Each time they met, he found her on his mind even more. The society women he met became paler, the idea of a future with one of them more uncomfortable.

She took another step away from him, and he felt another drop of rain. "Thank you for all you did for my father and me, and for the walk tonight . . . Mr. Winterton."

"You are welcome," he said, forcing himself not to go after her, not take her in his arms, not kiss her breathless as he'd done before. She was right; they needed to end this. It would be the hardest thing he'd ever done, but it was—as it always had been—inevitable.

He watched until she disappeared around the hedge, the cape heavy on his arm. She would return to her life as a maid in the baroness's household. He would see her when she served for the dinners he attended. He would marry someone else. She would bring them playing cards and add wood to the fires in the parlor to keep them warm.

He turned to the pathway and his life, some two miles to the west.

It started to rain.

Chapter Thirty-Two

Rebecca hurried back to the house to escape the quickly increasing rain. Thanks to the use of Kenneth's cape, she was still warm when she got inside. The lights were out in the kitchen save for the low lamp Cook kept burning all night.

Rebecca closed the door quietly behind her, then turned toward the staircase to the third level where her room was located.

"Mother?"

Rebecca jumped and put a hand over her mouth to keep from screaming.

Rose turned up the lamp on the counter. She was sitting on a stool. Waiting.

"Good heavens," Rebecca said, her heart pounding. "What are you doing up?"

"Who was that man?"

Rebecca's cheeks flushed hot, and she hoped Rose couldn't tell in the darkness. Her first impulse was to pretend she didn't understand Rose's question, but that would be unfair. Her next impulse was to lie, in fact Malcolm's name slid into place behind her tongue. It would be so easy to say she'd developed a friendship with the heir's valet and play out the lie Kenneth had started. It would be more comfortable for Rose if she told that version too.

Perhaps she better understood why Kenneth had lied when they first met.

"Rose," Rebecca said, trying to sound authoritative. "I am sorry to have kept you up. All is well, and I would like to go to bed."

"Who is he, Mother?"

Rebecca weighed her options a second time. How did Rose know she'd met a man? Had she followed her but not close enough to see who it was? Would she have recognized Kenneth?

Thank goodness they had not kissed tonight.

"I should like to keep my privacy on this topic, Rose."

When Rose did not respond right away, Rebecca risked a glance, surprised to see tears in Rose's eyes.

"It is not Mr. Timoltson, then," Rose said.

Mr. Timoltson? Rebecca hadn't told Rose anything about him because discouraging Mr. Timoltson was connected to Kenneth, and she had hidden everything about that association from her daughter. "I know you are concerned, but I assure you I am safe and I am well."

"Then tell me who he is."

"I cannot."

"Why?"

Why, indeed. "It is not often that I draw a line with you, Rose, but—"

"You *never* draw a line with me," Rose interrupted, coming to her feet. "You have always told me the truth, or at least I believed you had. Now you are hiding something? Why?"

"Because it is better you do not know."

"Why?"

Rose was the tenacious three-year-old again, unsatiated in her questions. Except she was not three years old. She was a grown woman with an understanding of men and women and what secrets might be kept between them. She was scared, and that broke Rebecca's heart, but to tell her the truth . . . How could she?

"Mama," Rose pled, her voice cracking. "You've been gone for well over an hour, and it is not the first time. You went out after dinner before and were gone too long then as well. I have tried to calm my fears, but you never keep secrets from me, and I am frightened by this one. I cannot think why you would not tell me who you are meeting, unless the answer *is* something I should be worried about."

Rebecca mentally debated her course for a few more seconds. Should she protect Kenneth and herself at the expense of Rose's well-being and the relationship they shared as mother and daughter?

Saying it that succinctly, even in her mind, made the decision an easier one. "It was Kenneth Winterton." Rebecca nearly bit her tongue after the name left her lips.

Rose's eyes widened, and she sat down hard upon the stool. "Mr. *Winterton*? The heir to the Brenston title?"

"It is a long story," Rebecca said, embarrassed as their unusual history flashed through her mind. "And not what you think."

"You do not know what I think," Rose said in an even tone.

Rebecca looked at the countertop, worn smooth by years of creating in this kitchen. She looked up with hesitation and met her daughter's eyes. "What *do* you think?"

"That my mother is being *very* foolish."

Rebecca laughed without humor. "That is true enough, but we only talked." *Tonight, at least.* And only because she'd promised herself she would not kiss him again.

"Mr. Winterton spent an hour outside *talking* with you?"

The unsaid accusation pricked Rebecca's spine. "Yes, he did."

"Are you in love with him?"

Rebecca gave another humorless laugh and shook her head, though she could not make her mouth form the words right away. "I am not quite *that* foolish, Rose. We met by accident, and it has been . . . complicated since then. We are friends."

"Friends?" Rose repeated in complete disbelief.

"Yes, friends. He made it possible for me to finish the silhouettes for the Brenston granddaughters. My father had not done any work past the original sketch. Mr. Winterton does not have many people he can talk to."

"And apparently neither do you."

They held each other's eyes across the counter, the lamp burning between them.

"Rose," Rebecca said softly. "Being your mother does not make me less of a woman in my own right. Though motherhood is my greatest joy, it is not all of me, especially now that you are grown. I have developed a friendship with a man out of my reach. That is not something a woman shares with her child."

Rose stood again, her eyes sad. She leaned forward and turned down the lamp until she was barely an outline in the darkened kitchen. "If what you have developed was only a friendship, you would have shared it with me."

She left Rebecca standing there with all the wrong words scattered at her feet.

Chapter Thirty-Three

"There you are!"

Kenneth looked up from where he'd been staring blankly at the book of accounts in front of him. It had been three days since the dinner party at Grangeford. Three days since he'd walked with Rebecca, but not kissed her. It had been a goodbye—her intention was to part as true friends—but it sat like a rock in his belly to think he might never talk with her that way again.

"Good afternoon, Lady Beth," he said. "What can I do for you?"

"I wanted to see how you were getting on. It seems you have been very busy this week." She settled herself into a chair across the desk from him and fixed him with her sharp brown eyes.

"Yes," Kenneth agreed, rolling the pencil between his fingers as he leaned back in his chair. "I have been going out with the steward to gain a better understanding of the lands. And meeting the tenants." Distracting himself with work had seemed like the best possible use of his energy, but it had proven not to be enough.

Lady Beth nodded. "The baroness is coming to dinner tonight, did you know?"

The baroness made him think about Rebecca. But then nearly everything made him think of Rebecca. "Um, yes, I do believe Lord Brenston informed me of that. It will be good to see her again."

He had only a vague recollection of the guest list. Every week seemed to have more social events than the last as part of Uncle Lester's goal to have Kenneth meet as many of the local women as possible. That thought made him think of Rebecca too.

"The baroness is a splendid conversationalist. She seems to like you quite a bit."

"We come from similar places."

Lady Beth furrowed her eyebrows.

"Oh, not geographical," he clarified. "I mean simply that we were both of lower circumstances before coming into our places."

"Oh, yes, however, she was a milliner's daughter. You were at least a gentleman's son."

At least. Kenneth's smile tightened but he said nothing.

Lady Beth did not notice his strained expression and continued, "There are a few more people coming—the Mortensons and Mrs. Greggory and her son."

"Excellent," Kenneth said. He liked Mr. Mortenson quite well. "It shall be a good party then."

"Mrs. Greggory is as fine a pianoforte player as any you have heard, I am sure. I have asked her to bring some music that could be danced to, and I wondered if I might ask you a favor."

She paused, but not long enough for him to speak before she continued. "Jacqueline shall have her season in the spring, you know, and she has, of course, been learning to dance since she was thirteen years old. Mr. Leliu is her teacher and says she is very skilled. However, she has not had many chances to dance with a partner. I wondered if you might take her to the floor tonight and help build her confidence regarding the steps."

"I am afraid I am not much of a dancer." While it was true he did not find dancing particularly enjoyable nor was he very good at it, the greater reason for his polite decline was based on not wishing to subject himself to Jacqueline's continued attention.

"That is fine," Lady Beth said, mistaking his refusal as acceptance. "She needs to be comfortable with partners of all levels of skill, so wherever you are on that spectrum will be perfect. Thank you so much. Oh, and please do not tell her that I asked. I want her to have the full experience of being chosen as a partner. It will be such a boon for her."

"I—"

Lady Beth stood and left the room before he could say anything else.

Kenneth sighed and scrubbed a hand over his face. A night that had promised some enjoyment sharing the company of the baroness and Mr. Mortenson was now resigned to be another evening tolerating discomfort.

He quietly criticized himself for being severe. Jacqueline's greatest flaw was her youth, and that was hardly her fault. He was her cousin—well, second cousin, or, rather cousin-once-removed . . . or something. He should support her coming of age as he would any family member.

It would be easier to do that if she did not continually try to flirt with him.

He returned to the ledgers with renewed determination. Rebecca would not be part of tonight's party, for which he was both grateful and disappointed. How could he want to see her while at the same time never want to see her again?

Their first meeting at the walnut tree had been an opportunity for him to apologize for his behavior and close their connection. Instead, he'd kissed her more fiercely than he had the first time. She'd returned passion for passion, desire for desire, and he still felt drunk from it despite the non-kissing encounters they'd shared since.

He groaned again and dropped his forehead onto his desk once, twice, three times. He did not understand his feelings and could not make sense of his inability to forget her.

Over the course of the next hour, Kenneth managed to make some headway on the ledgers, categorizing the last few years' sales of both livestock and crops and making a list of the men who used parts of the lands.

When it was time to get ready for dinner, he dismissed Malcolm, as he often did, in order to get himself ready. Malcolm took the day's soiled linens with him and left through the bedroom door. The rest of the house was set with servant entrances accessed by hidden staircases and back hallways no one in the main house would ever see. Kenneth thought of it as the backstage portion of a theater—essential to the production but created in such a way as to be unseen by the audience.

Kenneth liked that there was only one point of access to his room. It made him feel independent, even though he was as dependent as anyone ever was. On his uncle. On heraldry.

When he was presentable for the evening, Kenneth took the stairs that spiraled down from his tower without much energy. He was not in the mood to socialize, and even less in the mood to dance with Jacqueline.

He found little joy in dancing, yet it was one more aspect of a gentleman's life that he knew he ought to master. The woman he married would likely dance. The thought depleted even more of his energy.

He shook himself out of his moping before opening the door that led from the unadorned staircase to the well-appointed hallway filled with mahogany wainscoting, fine rugs, and framed artwork. He followed the sound of voices into the drawing room and put on his best society-smile as he entered the room.

He approached the first person he encountered—Mr. Mortenson—and said how nice it was to see him. Mr. Mortenson introduced the people he'd been conversing with—Mrs. Greggory, of the fine pianoforte playing, and her son, Mr. Greggory.

Mrs. Greggory, he learned through their introductory conversation, was widowed and a few years younger than he, which meant she was another prospect. He had not yet met her because she had been visiting family outside of Bath these last months.

Within a few minutes of being in her company, he determined she was educated and confident. She would make a fine countess, and he wondered if he ought to choose her simply to put the hunt to rest. Make his decision. Begin his new life. One woman would be the same as any other woman since none of them would be Rebecca.

When the conversation shifted, Kenneth excused himself and made his way around the room as Uncle Lester had taught him to do in order to familiarize himself with all the guests.

He felt his first moment of genuine gladness when he reached the baroness. He took her hand and brought it to his lips in greeting.

"It is wonderful to see you again, Mr. Winterton," the baroness said as he released her hand.

"As it is to see you, Baroness. I am glad you have not tired of my company enough to have refused the invitation to cross my path multiple times in a week."

"I enjoy your company very much, Mr. Winterton. And it has been some time since we have had so much society to partake of in Wakefield." She looked about the room that was filled with more than a dozen people. "I assume you are to thank for the increase of events on my social calendar."

"Yes, the thanks or the blame, depending on your view of it, is certainly upon my shoulders. My uncle wants me to meet the local gentry and begin building my place."

"I imagine he is primarily focused upon the *gentlewomen* of the county."

Kenneth lifted his eyebrows in surprise.

The baroness laughed. "It is the way of things, Mr. Winterton. Someone joins the ranks, and the first order of business is to find them a partner. Of course, most of the people in this room would never admit to knowing such a thing. It is one of those unspoken expectations of which, I can assure you, there are dozens."

He turned so he was standing beside her, looking out over the field of sparkling jewelry and tittering laughter. "One wonders how the unlearned shall ever divine them out."

"They learn," she said, taking a sip of her sherry. "They play the games and watch the races and set their pace accordingly."

"I wish I found that prospect more exciting than I do."

She lifted her eyebrows and turned to look at him. "You do not wish to marry?"

"I do not wish to marry for duty," he said, nodding his thanks at a footman who brought him a drink of his own. "My uncle has been very clear that in order for me to take my proper place, I shall need an appropriate wife to support my position."

"There are many fine women who would offer that very sort of support," the baroness said, looking back over the crowd. "I count three in this room."

He was glad she did not seem to count Jacqueline, which validated his opinion of not counting her either.

"And you are not intrigued by any of them?"

He chose not to answer.

The baroness followed his lead, and they stood in silence,

sipping their drinks and watching the glittering crowd. Lady Beth had her head bent toward Mrs. Greggory, who nodded thoughtfully as she listened to whatever it was Lady Beth had to say.

A young woman entered the room, looked around and then smiled when she saw the baroness. As she moved in their direction, Kenneth recognized something familiar in the girl, though he was certain they had never met.

"Ah, excellent," the baroness said when the young woman reached them. "Mr. Winterton, let me introduce my companion, Miss Rose Parker."

Kenneth tried not to stare. She had darker hair than her mother, and she stood a few inches taller, but the set of her shoulders was familiar. And she had the same bright green eyes that seemed to be boring a hole into him.

He realized a second too late that he was staring, and he quickly took the hand Rose offered so he might bow over it. He would have never guessed Rose had not been raised in this level of society; she had the poise and the manners well in hand.

"A pleasure to meet you, Miss Parker."

"Oh, I assure you the pleasure is all mine, Mr. Winterton. I believe you know my mother."

Chapter Thirty-Four

Y ou know Rose's mother?" the baroness asked, turning her full attention to Kenneth. Rose made no attempt to rescue him from the discomfort.

"Uh, yes, she and I have met. She, uh, well, her father did the silhouettes of the Brenston granddaughters." He waved toward the wall where the silhouettes were on display.

The baroness looked toward them. Rose continued to stare at him with such fierceness that he wondered how much she knew. Based on her expression, if she had happened to have a cricket bat in hand, he had no doubt she'd be pummeling him with it.

"Oh, that is remarkable," the baroness said. "I cannot believe I hadn't noticed those. I remember now, Rose, that your grandfather is a silhouette artist. What a happy coincidence that Mr. Winterton knows your family."

"Yes, happy indeed."

Kenneth shifted his weight awkwardly, feeling as though Miss Parker's eyes were about to light him on fire.

"Mrs. Parker has recently come to work in my household," the baroness continued, not seeming to sense the tension between Kenneth and her companion. "She worked there before Rose was born."

"Yes, I believe she mentioned that." He said it so Rose would hear that he *knew* her mother. That they had talked about their lives. It did not seem to lessen the hardness of her look, however.

"Oh, you know her well, then?" the baroness asked.

Kenneth was stepping into dangerous territory. He did not know what Rose knew, but he had an idea of what she *thought* she knew. "She and I have crossed paths on a few occasions." It felt good to be honest. "I think very highly of her."

The baroness lifted her eyebrows, and he felt the question there. He felt very highly of a servant in the baroness's household? That was not done. It was not *acceptable*. However, his words changed something in Rose's face, added a question that brought him some relief from her unblinking glare.

She looked away—finally—and he felt as though he could breathe. His brain spun, trying to find something else he could say that would further appease Rose without raising the baroness's interest in this topic overly much.

Dinner was announced before he had the chance to find those perfect words, which was as much salvation as it was a frustrating delay. Uncle Lester was one for ceremony, and the guests arranged themselves in order of rank, men leading women into the dining room. Kenneth was paired with Lady

Beth but struggled to be attentive to her conversation regarding Jacqueline's new gown and Mrs. Greggory's ruby pendant.

Mrs. Greggory was seated to his left, and he enjoyed conversing with her. He admired her confidence and, as she had lived in Wakefield all her life, she had a great deal of knowledge about both the area and the people. Was she perhaps showcasing her knowledge more than she would otherwise? Kenneth remembered how she and Lady Beth had had their heads together earlier. Perhaps Lady Beth had reminded Mrs. Greggory what it was Kenneth was supposed to be looking for in a wife?

How he hated this marriage mart he was hung within. So very much. The only viable solution to get out of it was, in fact, to marry.

Rose was seated a few places to his right, on his same side of the table, which he appreciated since it meant he could not see her and be reminded of Rebecca, though he never seemed to forget about Rebecca.

Uncle Lester and the baroness were seated beside one another at the head of the table and, in between his own additions to the conversation with Mrs. Greggory, Kenneth found himself watching them. Uncle Lester's face was different, lighter, and he laughed more freely in the baroness's company. Uncle Lester had been friends with the late baron, but was there perhaps something more than that between them now?

Dinner concluded, and the men enjoyed their port before joining the women in the drawing room. Mrs. Greggory was already at the piano, and most of the furniture had been pushed to the side, which meant the dancing would begin soon. Kenneth had formulated a plan during the course of the meal and made his way toward Rose with as much intention as possible without drawing other people's notice.

She was talking with the young Mr. Greggory but excused herself when Kenneth approached. She stepped toward him and lifted an eyebrow expectantly.

"At least smile so that anyone watching will not wonder what it is we are talking about." He smiled for good measure.

"It seems you know how all the games are played," Rose said, though she smiled slightly too. It did not reach her eyes, and he was again grateful she did not have access to a cricket bat.

Lady Beth clapped her hands, and the group turned toward her as she announced the dancing portion of the evening. Kenneth groaned inside, thinking his chance to talk to Rose was gone, but Mr. Greggory stepped up to Jacqueline as soon as Lady Beth had finished the announcement. Jacqueline smiled back at him as she took his hand.

Kenneth now had a full set's worth of time to talk to Rose. He waited until four couples were lined up to dance before he spoke to her again.

"It is not what you think," he said under his breath, looking around to make sure no one could overhear them. The attendees who were not dancing were watching the merriment and not paying any attention to them. The baroness was laughing at something Uncle Lester had said. Uncle Lester was laughing, too, which distracted Kenneth for a moment.

"Perhaps it is not what *you* think," Rose said with all the confidence of a debutante, successfully drawing his attention back to her.

He glanced at her only to find she was staring him down again.

"My mother is as solid a woman as you will ever know, Mr. Winterton. She might not be of your class, but she is strong and brilliant and very, very good. She has never lied to me or withheld information from me until now. Why would she do that?"

"Perhaps because she knows you might jump to erroneous conclusions?"

"Conclusions that you are dallying with a woman you will never have in decency?"

Kenneth felt his cheeks heat up. "I am not dallying with your mother." Was he? What exactly did dallying imply? He knew his definition, but would Rebecca define it the same way? Would Rose?

"Then leave her alone," Rose said, fixing him with those green eyes again. "She can only lose at whatever game you are playing."

He held her eyes and felt the truth of Rose's words. Rebecca *had* been on the losing end all along. He should leave her alone, and he kept meaning to. But then she would appear in his life again, and he would need to be in her company again. And as soon as they parted, he was thinking about her again. Even now, the good conversation he'd had with Mrs. Greggory at dinner felt brittle in comparison to the conversation he'd had with Rebecca a few nights ago.

"I care about your mother," he said, feeling that it needed to be said. For Rebecca's sake if not to defend himself.

"Which is all the more reason to leave her be." Rose lowered her voice to a whisper. "I do not know you, Mr. Winterton, and I have no idea what your intentions are, but I know my mother. She loves whole and hard, and you will hurt her if you continue this any longer. Everyone knows you are to be married to one of the women in the county."

She waved her arm around the relatively small company, which was at least a quarter filled with eligible women.

Rose held his eyes and continued. "But you and I both know where that will leave my mother. Let her have her dignity and her freedom. If you truly care for her as you say you do, end whatever it is between you. Now."

Chapter Thirty-Five

Even after the baroness took Rose to the other side of the room to meet the Marksons, Kenneth could not stop thinking of what she'd said. Whatever had been between Rebecca and himself was over. Their separation at the walnut tree on Thursday night had been the end of things. So why had he not said so to Rose? And why did the consideration of saying it feel wrong?

A quiet voice inside him answered that it was because he was still hoping things weren't over with Rebecca. That was dangerous. For his heart, yes, but even more so for hers. She'd always had more to lose than he did, which meant Rose was right. If he cared for Rebecca, he would not pursue her.

"Jacqueline is free for the next set."

Kenneth startled and looked to his side. When had Lady Beth come to stand beside him?

"Of course," he said, looking about the room to locate

Jacqueline. She was dancing with a young man he did not know. "Though it does seem as though she's had plenty of partners. Perhaps she no longer needs her uncle to help her feel confident."

"You are not her uncle," Lady Beth said with a laugh in her voice. "And it is a great benefit for her to dance with a variety of eligible men as she finds her way."

Eligible. It was an interesting word for Lady Beth to use, and it hit something in his mind like a hammer as he watched her walk away from him.

He had interpreted Jacqueline's actions toward him these last weeks as those of a young girl with a crush, but was he missing a larger plan in play? Kenneth watched Lady Beth; she engaged in conversation but her eyes remained on Jacqueline. He thought of their conversation in the hall that night several weeks ago, where she'd asked him about his prospects and his desire to marry a true partner. He'd thought she'd been an ally.

The current set was ending, and Kenneth slipped away to the other side of the room where he struck up another conversation with Mr. Montgomery. When the set finished, Jacqueline's current partner bowed over her hand and stepped aside. She put her head together with one of her friends in attendance, smiling and giggling as young girls did.

Kenneth surveyed the room and caught sight of a young man making his way toward her, his intention clearly to ask Jacqueline to dance. When the potential partner reached her, she looked past him, searching the room until her eyes met Kenneth's, almost as far away from her as he could be.

He did not look away and instead nodded toward the young man, indicating that she should accept the dance. She looked uncomfortable for a moment, but then her training rose up, and she turned to the would-be partner with a smile and a curtsey. He led her to the floor, and Kenneth relaxed. He looked at the clock.

The party had been dancing for over an hour; there would likely not be many sets left. Kenneth made a decision. He would be attentive to Jacqueline in case she was not asked to dance, at which time he would step in, but if she were well supplied with partners, which it seemed she was, he saw no reason why he should interfere. Especially if there were some machinations afoot that would only further complicate things within the household.

Lady Beth had asked him not to tell Jacqueline that she had suggested he ask her to dance. Yet it felt as if Jacqueline had been expecting him. Thinking that he had been manipulated sparked a fire in his belly, or, rather, fueled the fire already there—the fire that had burned since his life had moved out of his hands.

He could accept Uncle Lester's goals for him; his uncle had a duty to the title and had lost a great deal when Edward had died. Lady Beth's motivation was different. More cunning. More self-serving. Yet it made so much sense.

If Kenneth married Jacqueline, she would become the countess of Brenston. Uncle Lester's family line would be somewhat preserved, and Lady Beth's place would be secured at Brenning Hall. All the comforts the family had become accustomed to would remain in close to present condition.

Kenneth imagined Lady Beth coaching Jacqueline on how

she should interact with him, what she should say, how she should say it, and he suddenly felt very alone here, a naïve man who did not understand the part he played in the games of so many people.

"You have not danced tonight."

He startled, not having realized the baroness had approached him. He shook away his self-pity and found it easier to smile at her than it would have been to smile at some of the other guests. "I am not much for dancing."

The baroness tapped her cane thoughtfully in front of her. "Lady Beth said you would be dancing with Jacqueline."

Why would she have told people that? Kenneth wondered, but her reason was obvious now. "If Jacqueline lacked for partners, I would have," he said simply. "She has been very well received, however, so I did not feel the need to trouble myself."

"I am surprised she has not yet had a season in London," the baroness commented.

"She shall in the spring."

"She will be nineteen years old by then, still within the appropriate age, of course, but unusual. Especially for a girl so well connected as she is. I understand she was expected to have her season two years ago, but it was delayed due to Edward's tragic passing."

Kenneth pondered on that. Edward had been killed in July of 1816. Jacqueline's season would not have begun until after the traditional six-month mourning period had been observed.

He barely remembered Jacqueline from those early visits after Edward's death. She'd been so young, and he had been so overwhelmed by all that had changed. Why would Jacqueline not have had a season as soon as possible? She was the oldest of three girls—Cynthia's season would be delayed for Jacqueline's delay. Had Lady Beth been grooming her oldest daughter as a match for him from the start? The thought was repulsive in its possibility.

"I wonder, Mr. Winterton, if I might ask a favor."

He turned to look at the baroness, glad for something else to focus on. "Of course, my lady."

"It has been an age since a handsome young man has taken me for a ride in an open carriage, and I would so like the opportunity. Do you think you could accommodate such an excursion with me this week?"

"I'm certain I could," Kenneth said with feigned thoughtfulness. "Any young man in particular you would like for me to arrange? Mr. Greggory is easy on the eyes, I believe." He grinned at her.

She laughed and tapped her cane against his leg. "I am referring to your company, of course."

"I am hardly a young man," Kenneth said.

"You are hardly an old one, and you are younger than I am, therefore you fit the category."

"Well, in that case, I would be pleased to accommodate your request. Would Wednesday be to your liking?"

"Wednesday would be perfect," the baroness said. "I shall see you then."

Rose approached, throwing another glare in Kenneth's direction for good measure. "Are you ready, Baroness?"

Kenneth looked surprised. "You are leaving?" It was barely eight o'clock.

"I am not one for late nights when not entertaining in my own home," the baroness said, patting his arm. "I shall look forward to Wednesday."

He said good night, but whatever patience he had for the evening seemed to leave the room with the baroness and Rebecca's daughter. The laughter sounded too loud, the orchestra out of tune. He looked around the room of people and found very few that he wanted to spend any time with at all. The more he thought about his situation, the more he found himself unable to stomach the company.

Lady Beth caught his eye; her drawn mouth and direct look showed that she was not happy with him. He held her look with an equally displeased expression of his own and finished off his glass of scotch before setting the empty glass on the sideboard. Without bidding anyone farewell, he headed for the parlor door. It was not the first time he'd thought about leaving a dinner party early, but it was the first time he'd actually done it.

The music and laughter became more and more distant as he headed to his room, undoing his cravat along the way. When he stepped into the staircase and let the door close, all other sound disappeared completely. He closed his eyes in the reverberating silence.

He was heir to the earldom.

He would become the seventh Earl of Brenston.

Kenneth Bartholomew Winterton would be an afterthought.

Was there any point in attempting to preserve his identity or his independence within this place life had brought his way?

Did he even stand a chance?

Chapter Thirty-Six

Lady Beth found Kenneth alone in the breakfast room the next morning. She usually had a breakfast tray delivered to her room, but then he had been expecting this, so it did not surprise him overly much.

He stood as was polite and waited for her to sit down, but she stayed standing, staring at him without a glimmer of softness in her angled face. As was protocol, he remained standing too.

"Good morning, Lady Beth."

"How dare you snub my Jacqueline."

"I did not snub her," he said in an easy tone. "I watched to make sure she was partnered for each set, and she was."

"I asked you to dance with her, and you said you would."

"I actually said that I was not a very good dancer, and you took that as an agreement. I did plan to step in if needed, but I felt it far better for her to partner with eligible men than waste a set with her old cousin who barely knows the steps."

Did she catch his emphasis on *eligible*? He held her gaze though it was uncomfortable. Her eyes seemed to burn through him much as Rose's had last night. He seemed to have quite the knack for making women angry with him, starting with Rebecca. Though he did not think she was angry with him any longer. Not that it mattered.

Several seconds passed. He continued to stand and hold her gaze.

"I had asked *you* to dance with her. It would have shown her well."

"She shows well on her own, and I would hate for anyone to mistake my attention as interest, especially Jacqueline." *Or her mother*, he wanted to add, but did not.

Lady Beth's nostrils flared, but she said nothing, perhaps because there was little she could say without revealing herself.

Kenneth decided to take a step further and hoped he would not regret it. "I can see Jacqueline is working hard to develop the skills she shall need during her season next spring, but I hope it is clear to everyone that the *only* role I intend to fill in her life is that of an older cousin helping her to learn the steps and make the connections that will help her thrive if, in fact, my help is needed."

Two spots of color darkened Lady Beth's cheeks. She knew he knew. It was perhaps the first time Kenneth had seen her rendered speechless.

"I've no doubt Jacqueline will make a fine match, Lady Beth. You have every reason to be both proud and optimistic. Good day to you."

He walked past her, letting out a deep breath once he reached the hallway. He hoped she would not make their disagreement on this issue a lasting complication between them, but he had no regrets for having said what he said.

If only his other regrets would disappear, perhaps he could feel like a free man again. He dared not hope too much for what felt like an impossibility.

Chapter Thirty-Seven

This is very nice, Mr. Winterton," the baroness said once she was seated across from him, hands layered over the top of her cane. "It has been some time since I have ridden in an open carriage."

"For me as well," Kenneth said as the driver started the horses moving forward down the Grangeford drive. "My uncle finds them rather common, and it took some doing to convince him to allow the outing."

Kenneth sat facing Grangeford, and as the carriage drew him further and further away, he thought about Rebecca being inside those stone walls. What would she be doing right now? Did she know he'd been so close to her? Did it make her sad the same way it did him—to be so close and so distant all at once?

The baroness laughed, drawing his eyes from the fine house. "Oh, Lord Brenston and his extreme sense of propriety." She shook her head. "I keep telling him that old age is supposed to soften such edges, but he declares me out of place to say so."

Kenneth smiled. "You are the only person I have seen who pushes against his rigidity."

She shrugged. "I have known him the longest and have been pushing against those boundaries of propriety with him for a very long time."

"I understand your late husband was a good friend to Lord Brenston."

"They were quite close," she confirmed with a nod. "Lord Brenston was the elder of the two, but they came into their titles within a year of one another, and I think that created an important connection between them. After my marriage to William, your grandmother was one of the more welcoming gentry, for which I was very grateful. Lord Brenston ended up having no choice but to accept me as well, though I am quite sure I offended his sensibilities in the beginning."

"Offended?" Kenneth said. "That is a strong word."

"Indeed," she said. "And not one I use lightly. Can you imagine, given all his rules and manners, what he thought of his closest friend marrying a milliner's daughter? William never told me what Lord Brenston's reaction was, of course, but it was not hard to tell anyone's opinion when I arrived at an event on William's arm."

"I can only imagine," Kenneth said, thinking of how the local gentry would react to seeing Rebecca on his arm. He looked away to hide his expression of sorrow. It had been more than a week since he had last seen her, and reality was settling in that what they had shared was truly over. He would never talk to her alone as he had before. He missed her terribly, and the more he tried not to think of her, the more she snuck into his thoughts. The carriage passed the walnut tree, and he closed his eyes.

"Can you?"

He looked back at the baroness, confused. Had he missed a portion of their conversation?

She seemed to realize he'd gotten lost. "Can you imagine what it was like for me back then? Entering a room of my father's customers, knowing that most of them did not think I belonged within their circles?"

Kenneth nodded. He'd had a small taste of that when he'd come to Wakefield, feeling that people found him a poor substitute for Edward. "I can imagine it was very uncomfortable."

"Yet now I am respected and embraced as well as any other woman of title," she continued.

"Yes," Kenneth said, surprised at her bragging.

"I have the respect of the community, of my peers, and I have helped secure the barony in my son's absence. I have done quite well."

"Indeed, you have," Kenneth said, sensing that the baroness was leading him somewhere. He was glad to walk that path with her. "Do you ever marvel at the distance you have covered in that time?"

"Oh, yes," the baroness said, nodding. "A great many people have only known me in my current place, but I have never forgotten my history. That was perhaps the most difficult part to overcome—my feelings of inferiority and lack of confidence."

"It is hard to imagine any lack of confidence on your part," Kenneth said with all sincerity. He truly could not imagine the baroness with anything but full ownership of her role and position.

"And that is where William truly proved himself," she said, a wistful quality to her voice. "He never doubted my . . . I suppose the best word would be *worthiness*, within the position. He knew that I could learn the ways and do all I could to reflect well on him. And he was right. He did not share with me anyone's negativity and presented me as though I had every right to be there. In time, it seemed everyone believed him, including myself."

"That is remarkable," Kenneth said, wishing he'd known the baron. He sounded like a man well worth knowing.

"The first Mabon Ball was held on our wedding day," the baroness continued. "William broke protocol by hosting a ball for all the gentry in the county, inviting them to celebrate with us on the event of equal day and equal night." She glanced to the side. "Not many came to that first ball, as I recall."

Kenneth did not know what to say, though he wanted to ask if Uncle Lester had been in attendance.

She looked back and smiled at Kenneth. "And so William decided to throw the ball again the next year, and the next. I believe it took nearly a decade before we had more acceptances than refusals to our invitations. William was determined to see my position respected."

"Ten years is a long time to wait."

"Is it?" The baroness cocked her head. "We made a life in

between; I was not counting the days or the doors that opened to me. In time, the original purpose of the ball was forgotten, and the tradition simply reflected the joy of our lives together and the love of our community. That is why I chose to host it again this year. Even with William gone, our years together are worthy of celebration."

"That is wonderful," Kenneth said. News of the ball had been skittering about his new social circles for weeks, but none of the gossip held these important, personal details.

"Do you think you could do the same for your to-be countess?"

Kenneth startled at the quick change of topic. "Pardon?"

"Do you think you could help a woman feel confident about her place?"

"I have not chosen a countess," he said, feeling confused but also caught somehow.

She raised her eyebrows. "I'm not sure that is true."

Something tingled at the base of Kenneth's neck. The baroness looked intently at him from her side of the carriage.

"Baroness," he said after several seconds of silence, "if there is something you would like to say to me, I should be very grateful if you would be direct."

Rather than show surprise at his boldness, she smiled. "Excellent," she said, wriggling slightly in her seat. "I appreciate directness as well so I shall not mince my words. Are you in love with Rebecca Parker? If so, is she the reason you have not been able to find a wife?"

Chapter Thirty-Eight

The day of the Mabon Ball had arrived, and Grangeford had spent hours in a flurry of activity.

Except for Rebecca, who stood still outside the door to the baroness's bedchamber and tried to swallow her anxiety. She'd never been summoned to speak to the baroness in private before and could not think what she'd done to draw attention to herself on today of all days—the first guests had arrived nearly thirty minutes earlier. Her throat was dry by the time she worked up the courage to knock.

"Come in."

Rebecca pushed open the door and stepped just inside the doorway. "Mrs. Lenning said you wanted to speak with me, my lady?"

The baroness was seated at her vanity, putting light powder on her face. She turned on her stool and beckoned Rebecca to come closer. "Do come in, and close the door, if you would."

Rebecca followed the instructions, her heart beating. She could not think of what she'd done to warrant a reprimand. She'd worked hard to follow every direction she had been given since joining the household staff.

"I remember you, you know," the baroness said, looking up at her with a smile. "From when you worked here before."

Rebecca met the older woman's eyes but said nothing. Mrs. Lenning had said the same thing when she'd offered Rebecca the position, but it was still difficult to believe. There must have been a hundred maids since Rebecca had first worked at Grangeford. Why would the baroness remember one in particular who had only worked here for two years?

The baroness continued. "You were young, and fast. I believe you were in charge of the fireplaces." She lifted her eyebrows to indicate she was asking a question.

"Yes, ma'am."

The baroness smiled wider, and despite herself, Rebecca felt herself relax slightly. She did not seem angry.

"I remember you, in part, because the girl who came after you left ash on the hearth in the great room every morning for weeks. She never aligned the papers in the grate either. You were a fine worker."

"Thank you, ma'am."

"If I remember correctly, you left because you were to become a mother?"

"Yes, ma'am."

"And that child was Rose?"

Rebecca felt the warmth that always accompanied thoughts

of her daughter. There was still some tension between them after the confrontation about Kenneth. It tugged at Rebecca's heart to know she'd let her daughter down, but she had no further explanation to share.

Just as Rebecca must come to terms that her daughter was a grown woman with opinions of her own, she needed Rose to understand that she was more than just a mother. It felt a thin line to quibble over, since Kenneth was as out of reach as ever, but the point felt necessary to make. This new understanding of one another forming between them was important as they both made their way in new seasons of their lives.

"She is a remarkable young woman," the baroness said. "You have every reason to be incredibly proud of her."

"Thank you, ma'am. I am very proud. And so grateful for her place here. She has grown so much under your tutelage."

"I am glad, but she came ready to learn and do her best. That education is squarely in your ownership."

Rebecca smiled and nodded.

A silence fell between them, and Rebecca resisted the temptation to shift her weight.

"Do you know much of my story, Rebecca?"

Her story? She was a baroness. A fine woman in the county. But Rebecca sensed the baroness had more to tell her, so she responded as she believed she should. "No, ma'am."

"My father was a milliner—Richard's Hat Shop on Main Street. I doubt you would remember it."

"I do," Rebecca said, surprised by the information. "It had peacock feathers in the window."

The baroness's face lit up. "It did! My father had gone to India and brought those feathers back with him. He refused to ever use them for a hat, though many women begged him to do so." She looked to the side. "I have not thought about that for some time."

She laughed slightly, paused, then resumed the conversation.

"I expected to marry a man like my father, a man who worked with his hands and moved in merchant circles. And then I met William, and everything changed for both of us."

She looked directly at Rebecca, and Rebecca wondered again why she was there.

"Women like us do not believe in fairy tales, Rebecca. But there are times when circumstances do not follow the prescribed course, when the lines that seem so very solid turn out to be little more than a mirage." She paused once more. "Kenneth Winterton is a good man."

Rebecca felt a stinging behind her eyes and a tightness in her chest.

What did the baroness know?

And how did she know it?

Rebecca had been melancholy all week, ever since saying goodbye to Kenneth beneath the walnut tree, and now she was about to be fired. If that happened, her chances of finding another position in Wakefield would be significantly decreased. The stinging in her eyes turned to tears; she tried to blink them away before the baroness noticed. She stared at the floor, trying to control herself.

The baroness continued. "I have enjoyed getting to know

Mr. Winterton, and I believe he will do a fine job in his place when he inherits. He shall need a strong wife who will support him and help him find his confidence. He was not raised to this position, and there is a great deal for him to learn. He cannot do it alone."

Several seconds passed before Rebecca realized the baroness was awaiting her response. Her heart was in her throat for two reasons—worse than fear of losing her position was the knowledge that the baroness had discovered their connection and was reminding her of the sort of woman Kenneth must marry. The sort of woman *Rebecca* was not.

When the silence had stretched tight enough to snap, Rebecca forced words from her throat. "Yes, ma'am."

"Lord Brenston has made it a priority to introduce Mr. Winterton to every eligible woman in the county so he might find the woman who will best fill the position of wife and countess."

Rebecca's chest tightened like canvas stretched upon a frame. Once again, she was silent until she realized the baroness was awaiting her response. "Y-yes, ma'am."

"I agree with Lord Brenston that Mr. Winterton must find the right support—a woman who can withstand the discomfort of his position with him, learn with him, hold him up and make him better. I do not believe any man can fill such demands of title alone—certainly my William couldn't. And the entire county has seen what my son has done without a woman to help him find his place." She sighed. "That is neither here nor there. My point is that Mr. Winterton needs a strong support to make him into the man he can be. Part of the purpose of tonight's Mabon Ball is to bring every eligible woman into one place so he might make his choice in public and put an end to the speculation."

Rebecca's tears were for a different reason now. She'd been part of the preparation for tonight's ball for weeks. And it was where Kenneth would choose his wife? She had been storing coats and fetching trays for the invited women all evening. One of them would end the night on Kenneth's arm, and eventually become Kenneth's wife? How on earth would she stand that?

The baroness stood and walked toward Rebecca, who refused to look at her. She did not want the fine lady to see the effect of this information.

Rebecca could now imagine what had happened—the baroness had learned of their flirtation and wanted to make sure Rebecca understood the situation so she would be prepared. It was a kindness on the baroness's part, and Rebecca was sure that in time she would be grateful for the consideration. Right now, however, she only wanted to leave, find a corner where she could lose her composure for a few minutes, then brick her feelings back in and hope she could make it through the evening.

"He calls you Rebecca."

Rebecca's head came up, and she met the baroness's eyes.

"That was my first clue," the baroness continued. Her expression was gentle, and her smile was kind. "A few weeks ago, you brought him to the drawing room, and he said, 'Rebecca helped me find my way.' There was no opportunity for him to have known your name based on your interactions that night, and there was a different lightness about him. He watched the clock for the remainder of the evening and left early. According to Mrs. Lenning, you also finished work early—near the same time he did."

"My lady, I am so sorry," Rebecca said, her face on absolute fire. She would certainly be terminated for this, just as she'd told Kenneth would happen if their connection was discovered. And yet that thought was not overly uncomfortable. Right now, she wanted to be as far away from him as she could get. Leave her shame in Wakefield and find a new place altogether. She felt suddenly exhausted by the last few months.

"What, exactly, are you sorry for?"

"For being deceitful. For bringing disgrace on your household."

"Oh, Rebecca, you misinterpret my intentions of this meeting by a very wide margin."

Rebecca met her eyes once again.

"I am not an educated woman by any means," the baroness said, walking back to her vanity table and returning to the stool.

She looked at Rebecca in the mirror as she patted her hair again and began to put on the jewelry that had been set on the table.

"But I am intelligent. I am not silly, but I like to laugh. I am not ignorant of protocol, but I am, at my core, an absolute romantic."

She put one earbob on and then the other, looking between her own reflection and Rebecca's in the mirror.

"There are only a few people who know the true purpose of tonight's ball. Mr. Winterton—your Kenneth, as I understand he prefers you to call him—is, of course, very much aware that a statement is to be made. It was not his idea, mind you, I shall take all credit for that part, but he was in agreement that this was the best way for him to state his intention to choose you as his wife."

All movement in the room, save for the steady and rapid beat of Rebecca's heart, stilled. Had the baroness truly said what Rebecca thought she had said?

"As I said before," the baroness said as she pulled on her evening gloves of black satin. "He needs a woman who understands his position, but more than that, he needs a partner he can trust. With whom he can be himself. Someone who will grow with him and—"

"I am a maid," Rebecca cut in, wiping at a tear that had escaped her control.

The baroness looked at her in the mirror again. "You are the woman he loves. The woman he wants by his side."

Rebecca shook her head. "It was folly that we met at all and then let the energy between us become what it became, but that does not make it right and it does not make a . . . connection possible."

"I disagree," the baroness said, turning to face Rebecca again. "And so does he."

Another tear slid down her cheek. "I do not know what he has told you, but to assume anything permanent between us is foolishness."

The baroness raised her eyebrows. "Are you calling me a fool?"

Rebecca needed to make her point. "If you are implying

that the rising of a milliner's daughter to a baroness is the same as an artist's daughter rising to a countess, then I suppose I am."

The baroness' eyes went wide, and Rebecca looked at the floor again. "I am sorry, ma'am. May I *please* return belowstairs so I might finish my work?"

"Do you love him?"

Rebecca was unable to answer as quickly as she would have liked; the question was a sticky one. "No, ma'am," she said, because it was the right answer to give.

"Are you sure?"

Rebecca looked at her again. "I loved my husband, so I very much know what love is. And I know that it develops through shared lives, not flirtation. *Love* is not what I feel for Kenneth." She immediately realized she should have called him Mr. Winterton.

"What do you feel for *Kenneth*?"

Intrigue, connection, energy, excitement, curiosity. Did she love him? *Could* she love him after so short a time and so few encounters between them? The answers did not matter. They would only make reality more painful.

There was a quiver in her voice when she spoke again. "Might I *please* return belowstairs, ma'am? There is a great deal to do as the guests arrive, and my absence puts additional pressure upon the rest of the staff."

"He is in love with *you*, Rebecca," the baroness said in a gentle voice. "You are the woman he wants in his life, and he is prepared to make that statement tonight in front of the entire county. I want you to forget your place in this world and forget his. I want you to think about what it has felt like to be with him, to talk to him, to share your feelings with him. I want you to consider that it might very well be love that you are feeling, love that will grow through a shared life you have described but which can start exactly as it has. If the decision concerned only the two of you, would you want to be together?"

"That is not the only consideration."

"If it were," the baroness restated.

"It isn't."

The baroness sighed. "You are a stubborn woman."

"I am a realistic woman," Rebecca countered, holding the woman's eyes, though it was not easy. "There is *something* between Mr. Winterton and myself, I will admit to that, and we have both pursued it more than we should have, given our circumstances. I am accountable for my part in that as well. But it has been little more than fantasy." She swallowed the regret that rose from saying the words out loud. "We both know it."

The baroness looked at her for a few more moments, then stood. She turned to the wardrobe and pulled it open to reveal a blue gown very different than her usual personal style. The dress had a sweetheart neckline and sleeves that fell off the shoulder. The bodice was fitted while the skirt bloomed outward to create a full skirt.

The baroness brought the dress to her bed and laid it out, adjusting the sleeves so they lay even, then fluffed the long skirts over the end of the mattress. The candlelight in the room caught the sheen of the satin bodice, making the dress sparkle.

"I had this made for you." The baroness stepped back and

cocked her head slightly to admire the gown. "Rose gave me one of your dresses to use as a pattern. I chose blue because that is the color you were wearing the day Mr. Winterton nearly ran you over. When he told me the story, he said that dress may have very well saved your life that day."

She turned to Rebecca, her expression serious. "It was not easy to find my place in this world, Rebecca, and it will not be easy for you either. There will be objections, there will be frustrations and expectations and a great deal to learn, but when two people choose to love one another and work side by side, they can build something remarkable and, in their way, they change the world. I have lived that reality. I know the possibility can be true if you can believe it for yourself."

Rebecca stared at the dress. It was fit for a princess and finer than anything Rebecca had ever owned.

The baroness had ordered it made for her?

Rose had helped?

Rebecca took a step toward the dress, pulled by some invisible power as she more fully realized what the baroness's support really meant. She was making herself an ally because she genuinely believed that Kenneth and Rebecca could make a marriage work. Rebecca reached out hesitantly and rubbed the satin between her fingers. She looked up at the older woman who was watching her.

"Baroness," she said softly, "Kenneth has not professed such feelings as your efforts reflect. Is this your agenda or his?"

"It was my idea to have you here, tonight, and for him to make the statement that needs to be made, but he is in full support. At a quarter to midnight, the orchestra shall play a waltz, and he shall lead you to the floor to dance. When midnight comes, and the start of a new quarter begins, he expects to have you in his arms.

"Mabon is a celebration of equal day and equal night, a symbol of the harvest, which played a pivotal role in my own marriage. Kenneth is prepared to make a similar statement in front of everyone tonight. That is how deeply he feels for you, Rebecca."

"Dance with me? Amid all the attendees?" Her mouth went dry at the prospect. People she'd served dinner to and who would not recognize her on the street, women who had their eye on Kenneth.

"A life with Kenneth means you will be amid all those attendees a great deal. As I said, it will not be simple, but it is possible if you believe it. Kenneth already does."

Rebecca swallowed, feeling the warmth of Kenneth wanting her. "Why would he not tell me this himself?"

The baroness smiled and moved to her vanity, where she pulled a note from beneath her powder dish. She held it out to Rebecca, who looked at it a few moments before taking the sealed paper.

"If it is any consolation, being the center of attention and making such a dramatic statement is not in his nature any more than it is in yours. But he understands that the presentation is important. There is no chance for gossip when nothing is hidden, and he wants to make a strong statement that is not misunderstood by anyone here tonight."

A dozen scenes flashed through her mind. The scowl of the

women who had salivated over the earldom. Her standing in a room wearing this dress. The baroness watching eagerly. Lord Brenston's face going red.

And then her mind settled on the image of Kenneth approaching her, putting out his hand, bowing over hers, and walking her to the middle of the floor. Looking only at her. Touching only her. Knowing that he could have had any choice in the room, and he'd chosen *her*. The rush of calm she felt surprised Rebecca.

"I need to attend to my guests," the baroness said, moving toward the door. "My ladies' maid is waiting to help you dress if you decide to take this step."

"Decide?" Rebecca said, staring at her name scrawled upon the letter in her hand. She had the oddest sensation of being exactly where she was supposed to be. She'd felt the same when she reflected on the day she and Kenneth had met—and kissed—on the side of the road.

"The choice is yours, Rebecca, and if you are unable to choose the path that Kenneth is already upon, no one will fault you, and no one—aside from you, me, Kenneth, and Rose— will ever know. We are not taking away your agency in this, but I sincerely hope you will not allow class and circumstance to deny you both of what I think can be a beautiful life together."

She left Rebecca alone in her bedchamber, the blue dress ready and her own ladies' maid only a bellpull away. For several seconds, Rebecca stayed right where she was, holding the letter, looking between the door and the dress while fear and confusion circled and roiled in her chest. Finally, she sat down on the bench at the end of the bed, took a breath, and opened Kenneth's letter.

Dearest Rebecca,

I do not know how this letter will have been presented to you, but I can guess at your reaction. Surprise and perhaps some confusion. We have had so little time together, but that is exactly what I hope to resolve tonight. I have known since my arrival in Wakefield that my first responsibility is to the earldom and, in keeping with that allegiance, to find a wife amid the eligible women of the local gentry. I have met them all, and they have all been forgotten as soon as they leave the room.

You are the woman I cannot stop thinking about, wondering for, worrying over. The time we have spent together has resulted in the most enjoyable moments I've had in many years—even when that time together resulted in bruises from thrown walnuts.

I love your strength of character, your ability to love deeply and thoroughly. Your talent in blending light and shadow to create a silhouette worthy of the highest courts is astounding, and yet I know you do not undertake the work for praise, but for personal satisfaction.

You always seem to be so comfortable being yourself in whatever situation you find yourself. As one who rarely feels such confidence in shouldering my new responsibility to the earldom, I have drawn strength from your example.

I have been alone for so many years, then I met you, and now the thought of returning to that solitary life is unthinkable. You have shown me that there is still much joy and excitement to experience. It is my deepest hope that I might be the one to share that life with you.

I simply cannot marry any other woman as it would be vastly unfair to her, because I am in love with you, Rebecca, and though it seems impossible to imagine it, I think you might be in love with me as well.

With the baroness's help, I have overcome my hesitations that you and I could make a match, and I would like to use tonight's ball as an opportunity to announce that intention to the world—or at least the gentry of Yorkshire. Such displays are against your nature, I know, and vastly uncomfortable, but as I am meant to take a public position, I feel it an important reflection of what life will be for us. We shall be watched. We shall be judged. But we shall be together, and I promise you that I shall do all in my power to give you a happy and comfortable life by my side.

If you agree with my intentions, I pray you will wear the dress the baroness has provided and present yourself to the ballroom at 11:00. At 11:45, the orchestra shall strike up a waltz, and I shall bow over your hand as I request the first dance of the rest of our lives.

If you are not agreeable to this, please send a note so I might be prepared when I arrive.

I shall respect your decision, though I remain,

> *Ever hopeful,*
> *And always yours,*
> *Kenneth*

Chapter Thirty-Nine

Kenneth heard the door open behind him but did not look up from his task. He'd all but mastered getting ready by himself, but was grateful that Malcolm, who did very little as his valet, had chosen to check on him tonight. He was all thumbs the closer it came to the time the household would leave for the ball.

"Thank goodness you've come, Malcolm, these blasted cuff links are testing my last nerve."

"Malcolm is indisposed."

Kenneth spun in surprise, and the cuff link fell to the floor. "Lady Beth," he said, grateful that he'd put his dress pants on a few minutes earlier. "This is an, uh, unexpected visit. Is everything alright?" She had never come to the tower room; no one did aside from Malcolm and the maids.

She stayed by the door, her expression difficult to read. Angry? Annoyed?

"Are you involved in a flirtation with a maid at Grangeford?"

His breath caught in his throat at the direct question, and rather than say something he would regret, or be unable to retract, he chose the wiser course—delay.

"I, uh—" He began to search the carpet for the dropped cuff link in hopes his brain would think of a suitable answer. He spotted the golden clasp a few feet away. Bending down to pick it up gave him the extra time he needed. Standing, he met Lady Beth's eye.

"I am certain you do not mean to pry into my personal affairs, Lady Beth."

"You are then? The rumors are true." She made a sound of disgust low in her throat. "My ladies' maid heard it from a member of staff at Grangeford. She said that you have been meeting in secret and plan to make an announcement tonight at the Mabon Ball. Is that true?"

Kenneth drew himself even straighter and taller. "It is inappropriate for you to ask me such a question, and I would like you to leave my bedchamber. I shall meet you at the carriage in a few minutes."

Instead of leaving, she came further into the room, circling him toward the fireplace as though she were trying to corner an animal. The room was round, however, and he stood nearly in the center of it.

"Inappropriate?" Lady Beth said, two sharp spots of pink growing on her cheeks as she stopped in front of the mantel. "You have refused my daughter in deference to a *servant*, and you will school me on what is and is not inappropriate?"

"Yes," he said with a nod. "As I have told you, I will make a decision that feels right to me."

"My father will disinherit you."

"That is not a decision he can make, Lady Beth."

"He will most assuredly run you out of Brenning Hall."

"I suppose that is possible," Kenneth said, keeping his voice as calm as he could manage though his heart was racing. "I have no desire for ill will between us, Lady Beth, but I will be my own man when it comes to who I promise my life to."

He held her eye a moment and then turned to his mirror to work on the cuff link, hoping she couldn't hear the thudding of his heart over the sound of her swishing skirts as she left the room. She slammed the door hard behind her exit.

Kenneth thought back to the lecture Uncle Lester had given him early on about claiming his place and expecting people to respect it. Kenneth did not think this was the situation in which Uncle Lester would hope to see him stand up for himself, but Kenneth couldn't think of a better place to start.

His thoughts transitioned from Lady Beth's frustrations to the night ahead. The baroness had promised him she would have Rebecca there. And he believed she would make good on her word. What he would say to Rebecca, and what she would say to him, remained to be seen, but he was choosing to have faith that all would work out. He'd made his decision; tonight was simply the opportunity to share that decision with the rest of Yorkshire.

The. Rest. Of. *Yorkshire.*

He swallowed against the building anxiety.

Uncle Lester could not have Kenneth disinherited without an act of parliament, but he *could* bar him from Brenning Hall and make the transition difficult. He could defame both Kenneth and Rebecca to the degree that when the time came for Kenneth to take his place, the entire county was turned against them. That would change everything.

And yet, everything had already changed when Edward died. Kenneth was already viewed as an outsider. His accent was different. His manner was not quite right. And he was not happy envisioning the life that Uncle Lester demanded of him.

It was easy for those on the outside to see that all of Kenneth's fortunes had improved, but "improvement" was a subjective determination in some accounts. The greatest improvement he had discovered amid all the changes laid at his feet was that he'd met Rebecca. He'd been content in his life before the title had shifted to his shoulders, and he did not doubt he could be even more so with Rebecca beside him—even if that were in Sussex on a small estate that afforded few luxuries. Luxury was a subjective determination, too.

He finally locked the cuff, slid into his perfectly fitted jacket and looked at himself from all angles. *Not bad*, he decided with an encouraging smile, though his stomach was not yet settled. It would be an uncomfortable carriage tonight, riding with Lady Beth and her daughters, but he saw it as a minor obstacle. There would be a great deal of continued discomfort in the future, too. He was ready for it all.

He strode to the door, took hold of the knob, and twisted,

but the knob did not turn. He paused, then tried again. No movement at all.

He stepped back to inspect the heavy door with its equally heavy iron knob, studying the standard locking mechanism. That it was locked at all concerned him, but he did not let his mind wander down suspicious paths just yet and instead went to the mantel where he stored the key. These types of locks could be locked and unlocked from either side of the door.

The key was not on the mantel. Yet it had been right there a few days earlier . . .

Lady Beth had been standing near the fireplace when he'd turned away from her and asked her to leave. Would she?

Had she?

He had to take a deep breath before he could admit it to himself: Lady Beth had locked him in his room.

He almost laughed at the thought because it was so very gothic and ridiculous. She could not think that locking him in his room would change his feelings about loving Rebecca or marrying Jacqueline.

He took another breath and returned to the door, hands on hips as he surveyed the heavy wooden barrier. For the first time, he wished his tower room had a servants' entrance as the other rooms in the house did. He had only this single door set upon cast-iron hinges.

He banged his fist on the thick panel. "Open this door!" He pressed his ear against it, hoping he would hear movement on the other side.

There was nothing because he had chosen to take the tower

room, which was removed from the rest of the living quarters with only one entrance at the top of a spiral staircase. A maid came in the morning and evening, and Malcolm came at pre-arranged times. The fire was already set for tonight, and he'd given Malcolm leave to visit his friends at the pub in Wakefield for the evening. Which meant Kenneth could expect no one until tomorrow morning when the maid came.

He hurried to the window in time to see the lanterns of a carriage bouncing down the drive on its way to Grangeford. He opened the window and screamed and waved his arms, but no one saw him or heard him as the carriage carrying Lady Beth and her daughters disappeared into the darkness.

They were going to the ball—his ball—without him.

He continued to yell for help, but the front lawns remained empty. No one was coming to his rescue. He was four floors up, snug in this tower that had once made him feel so independent and removed. He checked his pocket watch. It was nearly 9:30. He'd planned to arrive fashionably late, but he had promised the baroness he'd be there by 10:00.

He went back to the door and set aside all his dignity as he screamed for someone to let him out. He was a grown man locked in a tower in order to prevent him from publicly declaring his intentions toward his true love.

He rolled his eyes at the ridiculousness of his situation, then banged on the door again. There had to be a way out!

Rebecca was waiting.

Chapter Forty

Rebecca stared at herself in the looking glass and swallowed. It was her reflection looking back at her, and yet it was a different woman entirely. The stays and the straps and the perfect fit of the dress were unlike anything she'd ever worn before. In fact, she was not sure she'd ever worn a *gown*. The blue fabric made her eyes look even greener.

Hansen, the baroness's ladies' maid, had twisted and curled Rebecca's hair into something soft and elegant. She'd shown Rebecca how to apply a thin layer of powder to keep her face from becoming too shiny beneath the lights in the ballroom. She'd offered some of the baroness's jewelry as well, but that was a step too far for Rebecca. The dress and the hair were all the transformation she could manage with any degree of comfort.

Comfort.

Nothing about this felt comfortable, but then she closed her eyes and imagined Kenneth waiting for her. Wanting to be with her. Willing to make whatever adaptations were required for them to be together, starting today, on this day of equality. It would be a powerful statement in front of everyone of consequence.

She forced the fear away and thought only of his intention and his hope—all of it expressed in the letter she'd read half a dozen times. She kept it tucked into the bodice of her dress in case she needed a reminder that this was really happening.

She opened her eyes and smiled as confidently as possible at the nervous woman in the mirror before turning to the door of the baroness's bedchamber, lifting her chin, and walking toward the ultimate unknown.

She'd taken two steps when the door burst open, startling her. She let out a little squeak and put a hand to her incredibly low neckline.

The baroness on the other side of the door was also startled. "Oh, my dear, I cannot believe I nearly forgot." She hurried past Rebecca toward the wardrobe, where she rummaged in the back before pulling out a box. She brought it to the bench at the foot of the bed.

"Shoes, my dear, are as important as any gown." She paused and looked Rebecca up and down. "You look lovely, by the way, just as I expected."

"Thank you," Rebecca said, swishing the skirt slightly to watch how fluidly the fabric moved. "My own slippers will be fine, I assure you. You should not have left your guests."

She poked out a toe from beneath her hem, showing the black leather of her shoe. She'd been given a pair of comfortable house slippers when she'd taken the position at Grangeford.

They were good quality, and an example of how considerate the baroness was toward her staff. Even before tonight, which still felt very much like an impossible fairy tale.

"Kenneth is not yet here, and you need to dress the part, head to toe." The baroness removed the top of the box and pulled out a pair of ballroom slippers. The sheen of the satin caught the light in the room, making the footwear look like polished silver.

Rebecca gasped. Like the dress she had not expected or the jewelry she had not felt comfortable wearing, the slippers were far beyond anything she had ever worn. "Oh, my lady, I could not possibly wear something so fine."

"You most certainly can. Kenneth picked them out especially for you. He wanted you to feel every bit the part of his future countess."

"But no one shall even see them beneath my gown."

"You will stand and move differently when wearing them. The other guests shall see that." She held the shoes out to Rebecca, who looked at them with trepidation. The baroness shook them slightly. "Go on, Rebecca. The soles are of the finest leather and shall feel like you are walking on cushions."

Rebecca still did not take them.

"I shall ruin them," Rebecca said. "I've never worn anything so fine."

The baroness held them closer to her still, shaking them again. "Now really, Rebecca, put them on. They will help you more fully enjoy this night. They are only shoes; it is not as though they are made of glass."

Chapter Forty-One

Rebecca entered the ballroom with the baroness beside her, struggling to breathe as she looked around the room full of people. It seemed that every woman there—and there were many—was dressed in an opulent gown and glittered with rubies and diamonds of all shapes and sizes.

Rose had been waiting near the door and stepped up beside her, looping her arm though Rebecca's. "You look beautiful, Mother."

"I feel very out of place," Rebecca said as they walked further into the room. Rebecca would eventually reprimand her daughter for not warning her of the baroness's plan, but for now, she would hold on and draw strength from Rose, who was more familiar with this type of place than Rebecca was.

"I felt the same for the first few times I attended such events," Rose said, giving Rebecca's arm a squeeze.

"As did I," the baroness said from Rebecca's other side.

They shared a smile, and then the baroness began introducing Rebecca to the guests scattered around the room.

"This is Rebecca Parker, a friend of mine who is joining us for the occasion," the baroness said to everyone they met.

The expressions on the faces of the other guests ranged from curiosity to distrust. No one knew who she was, even though she recognized several people from their positions of prominence in the county.

Perhaps because she was with the baroness, no one asked questions that could reveal her, and perhaps because she was with Rose, she kept her chin up, and her smile in place during what felt like an endless parade, with her at the head.

Between introductions, she looked for Kenneth, anticipating the moment he would see her. His note had said nothing about when to expect him, but she had thought he would have arrived long ago. Judging from the way Rose and the baroness kept looking toward the doors and sharing concerned glances, Rebecca was not the only one wondering why he was not yet here.

He would not have changed his mind, would he?

"Rebecca Parker?"

Rebecca turned toward the current introduction and felt her stomach fall as she looked into the face of Lady Beth. If anyone in attendance would recognize Rebecca, it was her or one of her daughters. They held one another's eyes for several seconds while Rebecca held her breath.

"Are you not a servant in this household, Mrs. Parker? Now that you are not apprenticing with your father?"

The section of the crowd around them went quiet, and Rebecca felt heat climb up her neck and cheeks. The silence turned to whispers as heads moved together.

"She is my guest," the baroness said, her smile stiff and her tone firm.

"And your servant," Lady Beth said without hesitation or deference to the baroness's position as mistress of the house. "You are humiliating every one of your attendees by bringing her here, Baroness." She waved her hand to encompass the room, not lowering her voice in the least.

"Me?" the baroness said, her voice calm and cool. "As this is *my* home and *my* party, I am free to invite anyone I like. If any of my attendees disapprove of my guest list, they are, of course, free to go."

Rebecca's face was flaming, and she wanted nothing more than to leave. Everyone was looking at her, watching her, whispering about her. Rose's grip on her arm was the only thing keeping Rebecca's silver-slippered feet planted on the ballroom floor.

She knew better than to show how she felt—though her face had already betrayed her—and so she focused on her breathing and keeping her spine straight and her shoulders back. Rose was right here. The baroness had made these arrangements. Kenneth would come. She was safe. Protected. And if she wanted to stand at Kenneth's side through the next decades of life, she needed to start by standing right here.

Lady Beth and the baroness faced off for a few seconds, then

Lady Beth nodded and dropped a small curtsy. If not for the hardness of her face, one might think she was conceding.

"Of course," Lady Beth said in a flat tone. She turned her icy glare to Rebecca. "I hope you are not too disappointed by the evening, Mrs. Parker."

She strode away, revealing a younger version of herself whom Rebecca had not noticed behind her. The girl stared wide-eyed at Rebecca with both open curiosity and thoughtful consideration.

"Good evening, Miss Cynthia," the baroness said as though the exchange with Lady Beth had never occurred. "Let me introduce Mrs. Parker. She is a guest of mine here at my invitation."

"A pleasure to see you again, ma'am," Miss Cynthia Marlow said as she dropped a respectful curtsy.

The first time Rebecca had met Miss Cynthia had been when the Brenston granddaughters had sat in Father's studio. Their most recent meeting had been on the street several weeks ago when the girl had greeted her outside the shops and looked on as she and Kenneth had conversed, perhaps not as discreetly as Rebecca had thought.

Like her mother, this girl knew exactly who Rebecca was. Unlike her mother, she was willing to extend Rebecca some courtesy. Unless she was simply doing a better job of hiding her distaste than her mother had been able to do.

"The pleasure is all mine, Miss Cynthia."

"I was very pleased with the silhouette your father did of my sisters and me," Miss Cynthia continued.

Rebecca felt Rose tense as she realized that they knew one

another, likely fearing it would end badly. But Miss Cynthia was keeping her voice soft and her tone neutral.

"I am glad to hear that, Miss Cynthia," Rebecca said, ducking her head in thanks.

Miss Cynthia smiled, somewhat nervously, then curtsied again and walked in the opposite direction as her mother.

Rose and the baroness shared a relieved look, which Rebecca tried to ignore. She looked at the clock. It was after 11:00.

Why was Kenneth not here yet?

"I cannot delay the dancing any longer," the baroness said quietly, before excusing herself and making her way to the small orchestra set in the corner of the ballroom.

Rebecca felt conspicuous without the baroness's company, but Rose was still with her, and though she could feel the surreptitious glances directed her way, no one was being outright dismissive toward her—other than Lady Beth.

Rose leaned toward Rebecca. "Where is he? He told the baroness he would be here by ten."

"Perhaps he changed his mind," Rebecca said, because someone had to say it.

"He would not do that to you or the baroness," Rose said with impressive confidence.

Rebecca struggled to feel the same surety; she'd read Kenneth's note and knew how he felt about her. Why would he go to all that trouble, promise the baroness he'd be here, then not come?

"He did not come with Lady Beth," Rebecca said as she drew the simple conclusion.

Rose looked confused, which prompted Rebecca to explain.

"Lady Beth and her daughters are here, but Kenn—Mr. Winterton, is not. Would they not have come together?"

"That is an excellent question," Rose said, then was silent for a thoughtful moment. "Miss Cynthia did not seem to share her mother's discomfort at your attendance here. Will you be alright on your own for a bit while I speak with her?"

"Certainly not," Rebecca said. Except for Rose and the baroness, there was not a single friend among the pretty faces. The baroness was in conversation with Lord Brenston at the —moment—when had he arrived? "Perhaps while you speak to Miss Cynthia, I shall find the Brenning Hall carriage driver."

Rebecca glanced at the large clock on the west wall of the ballroom—a clock she had dusted that morning. It was nearly a quarter after 11:00 now, and despite all her second guesses and insecurities, she did not believe Kenneth would have been late on purpose. In all the times they had met, he'd been on time or early. The letter he'd written showed his understanding of the importance of this moment for them. She could not believe he would forgo it.

Rose was reluctant to let Rebecca leave the room but eventually acquiesced. Rebecca made her way to the closest entrance, smiling and nodding at the people she passed on her way. She had never been the center of attention before, and she did not find it a comfortable place to be now.

As the ballroom doors closed behind her, she saw one of the footmen standing not far from her in the hallway.

"Nathan, thank goodness," she said, when she was close

enough to distinguish which footman he was. "I need some help."

"Yes, ma'am. I mean . . ." His eyes went wide in surprise. "Rebecca?"

After Rebecca explained her situation, Nathan led her to the front door. It had been raining, so before they left, Rebecca took off the slippers so they would not be ruined. She would risk her bare feet if it would preserve the slippers.

Rebecca held the slippers in one hand and her skirts in the other, not wanting to muddy the hem of the gown. It was Mabon, and the night was quite cool, especially in her thin gown with sleeves that fell off the shoulder.

She followed Nathan to the backyard where the carriage drivers were laughing and talking around a fire while they waited to take their patrons home after the ball.

"Who is the driver for Brenning Hall?" Nathan asked of the group that numbered at least forty men.

"I am," said a man, stepping forward, a glass of ale in one hand.

Rebecca recognized him as one of the Jensen boys—all of them were of an age with her and had gone into one sort of service or another. She'd not realized he was at Brenning Hall, but seeing a familiar face was a welcome kindness.

"Mr. Winterton—he did not come with your party tonight, Mr. Jensen, did he?" Rebecca asked, spurred forward by her growing concern.

"No, ma'am," he said, shaking his head. "Wasn't feeling well, I think."

"Wasn't feeling well?" a voice countered as another man stepped forward from the firelit faces. Rebecca did not know this carriage driver. "I drove Lord Brenston himself in time for dinner, and he assured me Mr. Winterton was coming later with Lady Beth."

"He musta come ill between your carriage and mine, then," Mr. Jensen said, shrugging his shoulders and returning to his seat on an overturned bucket.

The explanation did not sit right with Rebecca. The baroness had invited Kenneth to use the ball as the setting for him to announce his intentions. If he were unwell, he'd have found a way to tell her.

She turned her attention to the driver. "Did Mr. Winterton send a note, perhaps? To . . . um, me?"

"I dinna see any note."

She closed her eyes, feeling fear and humiliation compete in her chest. But she knew—she absolutely *knew*—Kenneth would not have left her in this situation. He'd meant to make a point tonight that she was his choice for countess. He understood the impact of that decision.

She opened her eyes and locked her gaze with Mr. Jensen. "Will you take me to Brenning Hall, please?"

A wave of surprise rippled through the men around the fire; a few of them laughed out loud.

Mr. Jensen didn't laugh, but he didn't stand up either. "Take *you*? In a Brenston carriage? They'd have my head if'n I was to—"

"Yes, he will."

Rebecca spun in surprise, then lowered her eyes as Lord Brenston approached. Rose was a few paces behind him and gave her mother a nervous smile.

"Something is afoot," Lord Brenston said, coming to a stop beside Rebecca and fixing his fierce look on the driver of his personal carriage. "Lewis, is the carriage accessible?"

"Yes, though it will take me a few minutes to bring it around, my lord."

Lord Brenston huffed and turned toward the driver of Lady Beth's carriage. "Jensen, where is your carriage?"

"Just there, my lord," he said, pointing toward a carriage on the edge of where the others were gathered. "We were one of the last to arrive."

"Excellent," he said with a sharp nod. He began moving toward it. After a few steps, Lord Brenston stopped and turned back to Rebecca. "Are you coming, Mrs. Parker?"

"Oh, um, of course I would *like* to come," Rebecca said, keenly aware of her bare feet. "I am quite worried about Kenneth."

Lord Brenston narrowed his eyes and harrumphed. "You shall refer to him as Mr. Winterton in company, thank you very much. There are ways things are done in certain circles." He turned to the carriage and began to walk. "Come, then, Mrs. Parker. We have things to discuss."

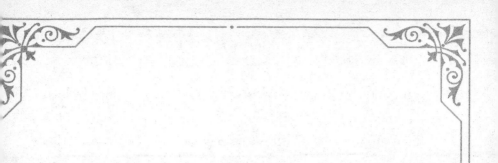

Chapter Forty-Two

In the hour he'd been locked in the tower, Kenneth had managed to pry out only one of the hinge bearings. It had taken a letter opener—which he broke—a shoehorn—which he bent to uselessness—and his dagger, which he'd forgotten he had until after his first two pieces of equipment failed.

He'd also poured an entire bottle of hair oil—found amid items stocked in his room but unused—over the hinge, which meant he was now covered in a sandalwood-scented liquid that made him feel light-headed. He was working on the second hinge when he heard carriage wheels on the drive.

The dagger clattered to the floor as he ran across the room to the window, which he had left open in hopes of rescue. He waved his arms and yelled, but the carriage did not slow as it disappeared under the portico. He cursed under his breath, slapping the windowsill with his oily hand.

Since no one seemed to hear him anyway, he vented his

frustration by yelling every curse word he knew—some of which he'd never spoken aloud before. If there was ever a night to use them, however, it was this one. He had never been this frustrated or incapable. What was Rebecca thinking?

He imagined her waiting for him, out of her element, trying to make sense of the words he'd written that he hadn't fulfilled. He felt sick to his stomach. Everything had been so intricately planned—except for Lady Beth and her pettiness. Her cruelty would not stop him, even if she could ruin the evening and orchestrate so much embarrassment for so many people.

He would get out of this tower eventually, and he would make his confession to Rebecca and Uncle Lester. If nothing else, wresting a 300-year-old door had only strengthened his determination. He would never forgive Lady Beth for preventing him from showing the world how he felt about Rebecca.

Even if he were freed from the tower right this moment, could he get to Grangeford in time?

It was nearly midnight. The orchestra was supposed to start up the waltz. He was supposed to take Rebecca to the floor.

Instead, he pictured the baroness, her jaw tight as she watched the clock. Lady Beth smiling with satisfaction as his moment ticked away. Rebecca, embarrassed and questioning his intention.

He had already asked for so much grace from her—could he expect even more?

He clenched his teeth and retrieved his dagger from the floor before putting the blade against the joint of the hinge. He was wriggling the blade back and forth, trying to force enough of a gap so he could pry the bearing when he thought he heard something on the other side of the door. He dropped the knife and banged both hands on the door even though he knew it would absorb most of the sound.

"I am here!" he yelled.

He needed to strike the door with something harder, something that would make more noise than his fists, which were already bruised from his prior attempts. He scanned his room, looking for something, anything.

"I'm locked in!" he yelled, finally moving toward the fireplace tools, prepared to pummel the door with the iron-handled pieces.

The door opened at the same time he turned around, the fireplace poker in one hand and the shovel in the other.

"Uncle Lester!" he said in surprise, dropping both instruments to the floor as he hurried toward his uncle who held what looked to be a ring of keys. "Thank goodness you've come! I need to get to Grangeford as soon as poss—"

He stopped walking, and his words were cut short as a vision in blue stepped into the room.

He met Rebecca's green eyes with his own. She was not at Grangeford wondering where he was. She was *here*, and looking like an absolute vision.

"Rebecca," he said in shock once his brain had recovered.

In the next instant, he was across the room. He took her face in his hands and kissed her soundly. "I'm so sorry," he said, pulling back a moment before kissing her again. "I had every intention of being there."

She took hold of his wrists, as she had that very first day, not letting him remove them. Her touch made him absolutely wild. He kissed her again.

"You look so beautiful!"

Kiss.

"I cannot believe you are here."

Kiss.

Uncle Lester cleared his throat, and Kenneth pulled back, looking at Rebecca's laughing green eyes, though she had not yet made a sound.

"Blast," he said under his breath. "I had forgotten he was here."

He stepped back from Rebecca and turned toward his uncle. Kenneth's hand found hers, and he held on tightly. He hoped he did not ruin her lovely gown with the oil on his fingers, but he was not about to let her go.

He noticed her bare feet peeking out from beneath her gown but did not have time to ask after it. He'd ordered beautiful silver slippers for the baroness to give her along with the dress, certain they would make Rebecca look and feel like a princess.

And when he had not been there to dance with her at the ball, she had come for him instead.

He squeezed her hand. She squeezed back, and it was all he could do not to kiss her again.

"Kenneth," Uncle Lester said almost like a groan. "You are the most maddening man I have ever met."

"Yes, Uncle," Kenneth said, nodding in agreement. He could take his licks because Rebecca was by his side, and he no longer cared what the outcome regarding his position would be.

Uncle Lester began pacing the tower room. "I have given you every opportunity—advantages other men dream of and never receive."

"Yes, Uncle."

"I have brought every eligible woman in the county to this house so you might meet them and see their quality."

"Indeed, you have," Kenneth agreed with a sharp nod. "Save one."

Uncle Lester furrowed his grizzled eyebrows.

"You never brought Rebecca to Brenning Hall," Kenneth said, tightening his grip. "I had to find her on the side of the road, in the baroness's dining room, and at her father's studio. In fact, I seemed to find her everywhere except here, even when I was not looking for her."

"And then you, apparently, *did* go looking for her," Uncle said.

It was Kenneth's turn to draw his eyebrows together.

Rebecca cleared her throat. "We came here in the same carriage. Lord Brenston and I had an interesting conversation."

"Very interesting," Uncle Lester said, resuming his pacing. "She claims you are in love with her."

Kenneth turned to look at her.

"Well, you did say as much in your letter," she said sheepishly.

"A letter meant for you," he said quietly.

"Oh, I was very upfront with her during our conversation, Kenneth," Uncle Lester said, glaring at Kenneth each time he turned during his pacing. "I told her without any margin of misunderstanding that if I were not convinced of this being a solid course, I would do everything in my power to prevent it." He stopped pacing and faced Kenneth dead on.

Kenneth swallowed, but he was not afraid of whatever sentence his uncle might pass upon him. "You cannot prevent this, Uncle."

Uncle Lester lifted his eyebrows.

"I will be with Rebecca, if she will have me, in whatever circumstance is available. As much as I want your favor and your training, if she will not be welcome here, we shall return to Sussex until such time as I inherit. But I *will* be with Rebecca. She is essential to my happiness, and I shall not apologize for that fact any longer."

"The earldom means so little to you?" Uncle Lester asked, sincere hurt in his tone.

"I do not mean to sound flippant about the title. I only mean to emphasize how much Rebecca means to me. Becoming heir changed my world, and I am determined to continue your legacy and secure the generations that follow us. You have said many times that I need a woman at my side to shore me up and help me become the man I am meant to be. I agree, completely, and I believe Rebecca is that woman. She makes me better. She makes me want to be better still."

"And if I deem her unacceptable as a countess?"

"With all due respect, Uncle, your opinion shall change the relationship we share and might influence my ability to work effectively in my position when I inherit, but I believe I have already stated my position rather clearly."

Uncle Lester harrumphed again and resumed his pacing, this time looking about the room as he did so.

"I hate this tower," he said, stopping to look out the open window, his hands on his hips. "It is cold and removed, and those stairs are not for the faint of heart. I want you to take rooms on the family level."

"A-Alright," Kenneth said. Was that the answer his uncle was looking for?

"I want you to host a dinner every week with the local gentry. It will help you get to know them and the needs of this county."

"Certainly."

"I want you to hunt and play cards and dance with my granddaughters when they need a partner."

"If I must."

Uncle Lester turned to face them and narrowed his eyes. "I want you to be a gentleman. Rebecca told me of your foolish attempts to go about town dressed as your valet. No more disguises, Kenneth. No more secrets."

"I will do my best to be the perfect gentleman, Uncle, but I must also be able to be myself. I can agree to no more disguises if I can be allowed to ride the horse I want as fast as I would like. I will hunt and gamble and dance if I might also sketch the landscape and design tenant cottages. I have absolute respect for you and for this position, but I will not completely give up the man I am. And I will not do any of it without Rebecca."

Uncle Lester waved his hand. "Oh, you may have Rebecca," he said as though that had been obvious. "If she will have *you*."

The clock in his room struck the first chime of midnight as Kenneth smiled at Rebecca. It was Mabon Midnight—the day of equal light and equal dark. She smiled back and gave his hand a squeeze.

Uncle Lester rolled his eyes and moved to the door. "Meet me in the study when you finish, and for goodness' sake, clean yourself up, Kenneth! You are an absolute mess."

He left the door open and disappeared down the stairs. Kenneth hurried to grab the hand towel and wipe as much oil from his hands as possible.

"It is midnight," Rebecca said when he returned to her. "The beginning of a new day."

He took both of her hands in his. "The first day of the rest of our lives, I hope. Equally yoked and equally measured." He could not believe she was here.

She lifted a hand to touch his cheek. "It will not be easy. For every Lord Brenston and the baroness, there will be a dozen Lady Beths set against us."

"But there will be you and me, together," he said, letting go of her hand so he could slide an arm around her waist and draw her closer. "You have already charmed my uncle, and the baroness is a fierce defender. I like our odds." He noticed her feet again. "Where are your shoes? I had ordered the most beautiful silver slippers. I wanted you to feel like a countess tonight."

"They are in the carriage," she said. "In the rush to reach you, I am afraid I forgot them, but they are beautiful, I assure you, and a very thoughtful gift."

He kissed her again; he couldn't help it. "You are here," he said in between the kisses. "I cannot believe you are here. We are together."

Rebecca laughed as he kissed her neck, then she pushed him back so she could meet his eyes again. Her expression softened. "What if I hold you back?"

"What if you make me the most successful Earl of Brenston ever known in Yorkshire?"

She smiled, but it quickly faded. He could see the nervousness in her eyes. "I am serious, Kenneth. I forgot my shoes in the carriage, I have more pins in my hair than I have ever worn before, and, quite frankly, they feel as though they are embedded into my skull. What if I cannot be who you need me to be?"

He leaned his forehead against hers and began to pull the pins from her hair, one at a time, letting them drop to the floor of his tower room. "You are exactly who I need, Rebecca. I love you. I want a life with you, however we can have it. If you do not feel the same way about our being together, tell me now. But if you feel for me what I feel for you, I believe we can build a beautiful life together."

Rebecca was silent a few seconds. It was difficult for Kenneth not to press his lips against her neck again, but he continued removing her hairpins—gracious, there were dozens of them. Finally, her hair began to fall in coils about her shoulders. Once it was completely free, he pushed his hands into it, feeling the strands slide through his fingers. Feeling the intimacy.

"Is that better?" he asked, pressing his lips against her hair, her ear, her neck.

"So much better," she said in a sultry tone that once again

spiked his energy. She pulled back so she could look into his face. "I want that life with you, Kenneth."

Every word completely thrilled him. "You do?"

She nodded. "I do. I am terrified, but I know how to work hard, and I promise I will do my best."

"Then today is the first day of our lives together, and I could not be a happier man." He pulled her toward the stairs. "My uncle is waiting."

She pulled on his hand, still clasped with hers. "Perhaps he could wait just a few minutes longer?"

When he looked back at her, eyebrows raised high with a question, she offered him a sheepish smile.

"It is always so much effort for us to get time alone to-gether," she said. "And without those pins giving me such a headache . . ."

He smiled and made short work of putting his hands back into that hair. And kissing those lips. And glorying in that fact that she was here. And he was with her. And after all this time, today was just the beginning.

Acknowledgments

Thank you, dear readers, for reading and sharing my stories. It makes what I do possible and helps me fulfill this part of my life and my purpose. Thank you to my kids; they have all grown up and are amazing (like Rose in this story) and have become my dearest friends. They have never stopped believing in me, and I will never stop being so very grateful for their support.

Thank you to Lisa Mangum and Heidi Taylor Gordon at Shadow Mountain who helped me brainstorm this book, specifically the idea of utilizing a silhouette artist, which was a trade I was unfamiliar with. They went on to produce and edit this book, which is why it looks so bright and shiny now. Thank you to the other people at Shadow Mountain who also put their hands toward the presentation of this book: Chris Schoebinger, Richard Erickson, Heather Ward, Rachael Ward, Troy Butcher, and Callie Hansen.

Thank you to Lane Heymont, owner and lead agent at

Tobias Literary Agency, for championing me and this story. I am so grateful to have him along my journey.

This story was inspired by the people I have met over the last couple of years who kept the faith of their own second chance and shared their stories with me. The belief that such fairy tales exist is what influenced this story the most, except for the knowledge that we are each here with a plan and a purpose. Sometimes there are turns in the road we did not expect, but God is still there around the bend, rooting for us and helping us find the way. I am so grateful for Him, for His love and His patience with me as I take those turns a little too fast sometimes and with too much fear other times. God is good. Life is good. Love is worth seeking.

Discussion Questions

1. Who was your favorite character in this story? Why?

2. The first kiss happened quickly in this story. Did you like the pacing of the romance or did you feel it was too fast?

3. Have you ever found yourself in an emotionally or/and physically abusive relationship? If so, did Rebecca's situation with her father resonate with you or did it miss some points you wish it had included?

4. This story looks at status in many ways—Kenneth's place in the new society he's inherited, but also the hierarchy among servants. What were your thoughts regarding Rose being positioned higher in the household than Rebecca? Would you be comfortable with that sort of situation?

5. What are your feelings regarding "Happily Ever After"?

6. In America, second marriages have a failure rate of 60 percent. Why do you think that is? If you are in a successful

second (or third, or fourth) marriage, what do you find are the biggest challenges?

7. How do you feel about balding men shaving their heads? For or against?

8. This story is a "second chance, secret prince, double Cinderella story." What aspects did you see in both Kenneth's and Rebecca's stories that match with the Cinderella theme?

About the Author

JOSI S. KILPACK is the author of several novels and one cookbook and a participant in several coauthored projects and anthologies. She is a four-time Whitney Award winner—including *Lord Fenton's Folly* (2015) for Best Romance and Best Novel of the Year—and a Utah Best in State winner for fiction. She is the mother of four children and lives in northern Utah.

You can find more information about Josi and her writing at josiskilpack.com.